the *Thorny Path*

Diana Elizabeth Tebbutt

Editing, design, typesetting and publishing by UK Book Publishing

www.ukbookpublishing.com

ISBN: 978-1-916572-78-2

the Thorny Path

With thanks to Tania for her help and support.

The Thorny Path

The path of life is full of thorns,
That erupt in full bloom each day,
They prick and prick and each sharp spike,
Draws blood along the way.

The thorns are hazards that come with life,
Sharpening their points with glee,
They leave a multitude of scars,
For all the world to see.

We bear the scars, we feel the hurt,
With fortitude bear the pain,
Because we know deep in our hearts,
The needles will prick once again.

How can we live with this we know,
How do we tread the path,
When knowing that if we do cry,
Others amongst us laugh.

We soldier on, just step by step,
Marching towards one goal,
And hope that by enduring such,
It cleanses our very soul.

DEL 2023.

Chapter 1

The Lancaster family were well known in the outskirts of Portsmouth. There were four children, three boys and one girl. The two eldest boys had joined the Merchant Navy and were seldom home. When they did return there was of course much celebration and rejoicing. Catherine was seven and in the junior school. Stuart was thirteen and at secondary school.

Mr Lancaster was an intellectual and provided a good home for his family through his teaching at a local college. Mrs Lancaster was happy not to work, do her cooking, potter around the garden and do embroidery and knitting.

One day Mr Lancaster, Percival, came in from work and said to his wife, "I have been offered a position as a lecturer in history at Harvard University in America."

"America!" echoed Mrs Lancaster.

"Yes, Harvard. I have been headhunted through a colleague who emigrated there. He has a position as Head of Year. He recommended me and advised me to send in my CV, which I did. They were satisfied at the university and happy to go along with his testimonial plus of course the CV."

Helen, Mrs Lancaster, was perturbed. They had lived in the area since marriage and she was happy here. She had no desire to emigrate to America.

The house they had lived in since marriage was on a peppercorn rent from Portsmouth College of Technology and if Mr Lancaster left it would no longer be their home.

"Are you really going to accept this position?" asked Helen tremulously.

"I am," replied Percival defiantly.

"What about the children's schooling?"

"There are schools in America, don't be so silly."

"But Stuart is doing so well and Catherine has only just gone into the Junior School. Stuart's teacher says he is exceptionally bright. His teacher, Mr Brown, thinks he should really be in a higher year group."

"You are being stupid, woman," retorted Mr Lancaster angrily. "America is not a third world country. I admit the boy is clever, he seemed to teach himself. He read at four, but the education system in America is well advanced."

"What about Catherine?"

"You are just putting up obstacles. She will be fine in an American school."

"I have my friends here," protested Helen. "I know I lost my mum and dad through cancer, but I have made many friends."

"People are people, woman. They do exist in America, you know. You will soon settle down."

"Where will we live?"

"Oh, accommodation will be sorted out by the university. I have heard there is a flat available. If it isn't suitable for you and the children, I will find you somewhere else."

Helen thought this all sounded rather odd. Almost as if her husband was going to be in the flat, and she, Catherine and Stuart would be somewhere else.

"What about our furniture and possessions? I have things I treasure from my parents. They are of great sentimental value to me."

"I have arranged for hauliers to come, take what we wish," explained Mr Lancaster.

"You have done all this without asking or telling me!" cried Helen angrily.

"Well, you always seem to be locked into cooking, housework and other trivial pursuits."

"Trivial pursuits! I have brought up your four children. Do you call that trivial?"

"You didn't seem to express much interest in my life at the university," said Mr Lancaster angrily. "All you seem fit for is being a housewife. You give me no encouragement. In fact, lately all you seem to concentrate on are the children. I can't discuss my work with you, and we don't even seem to have a decent conversation these days."

"Why did you marry me?" asked Helen tearfully.

"I was young, I suppose and wanted sex. You were pretty and when I met you at the church social you were the prettiest girl there. You seemed to have a sweet nature and

I fell for you."

"I am still the same person," said Helen.

"Maybe, maybe. I admit you are a good mother, but America beckons to me with the prospect of a more exciting life."

"But, we are coming with you, aren't we?" Helen asked tentatively.

"Yes, yes. I have booked your passage from Southampton. In fact, the boat sails in three weeks."

"Three weeks. How can I manage that?" cried Helen in horror. "I have to inform the school, and goodness so many more things."

"No problem!" said Percival. "All of my details have already been organised. Get a photograph of yourself and the children and I can fast track a passport. The school is no problem. Why, they just don't need to turn up. I have arranged for packers to bring boxes and help with the packing. I can sort out my own things myself. I have already organised quite a lot."

Helen was dumbfounded. It seemed as if an awful lot had gone on behind her back.

"Does anyone really know anyone?" she mused. She had thought that she and her husband were on terra firma, but now the ground seemed to be shaking beneath her feet.

Chapter 2

When Helen told the children, they were both bemused and excited. Stuart didn't want to say goodbye to his friends and Catherine really liked her teacher, but to go on a boat sounded exciting to the children, although they could see that their mother was troubled.

The time went quickly and the hauliers and packers did a good job. Helen was able to throw out some old things that they didn't really feel necessary, and Percival had already had his trunk packed and had told the packers to send some of his boxes into storage for the boat.

Helen had said goodbye to her friends and looked round the house that had been their home for many years. She remembered the happy times they had when first married and the joy when she had her first baby. She had felt that perhaps Percival had not really been as contented as before for some time, but put it down to a long marriage and that the excitement cannot really last for ever. She knew from her friends that marriage became more everyday, rather like a pair of gloves with which you become familiar, but she hadn't felt that anything was seriously wrong, and certainly no idea that Percival would ever leave England. His parents too had passed on, his father with a heart attack, soon followed by his mother who died, some said, of a broken heart. But he had always voted and seemed a true English boy. Helen wondered if perhaps she had become too housebound as it were, and not entered sufficiently into his college life. She had not gone to as many social events as perhaps she should, but he always seemed content for her to just run the home.

Chapter 3

The day came for leaving. There were still many boxes not collected by the packers, and Helen and the children were dressed for the departure. The passports had all been organised but Percival had not yet arrived. There had been a small leaving ceremony for him at the college, and Helen wondered if he had returned and was still saying belated farewells.

An hour before the taxi was due to take them to Southampton, Percival came in. He looked rather flushed and harassed. Helen was not surprised at this as there had indeed been a lot to organise for the departure.

"I am afraid I have something to say to you," said Percival rather sharply. "You are not going to like it and I think you had better sit down."

Helen was nonplussed. Surely they should be locking up and perhaps having a last look at the home that they had shared for so long?

"When we get to America, I shall not be living with you. I'm afraid I have fallen in love with another lady. An intellectual who is on my wavelength. You will of course all come with me, and I have found suitable accommodation for you near to Harvard. My lady will be with me in my flat. I shall of course ensure that you are financially provided for, but perhaps, Helen, you will eventually be able to find employment."

Helen felt sick. "Is the lady travelling with you to America?"

"She is. She was the bursar at the college and she too is going to work at Harvard."

"I can't possibly come with you under these conditions," gasped Helen. "Whatever are you thinking of? I'm not a pawn or a chess piece that you can move around at will. I have never been very happy at the thought of leaving England. I was born and brought up here, and raised my children here. Were you planning on having the equivalent of two wives in America?"

"No, my dear. I'm afraid that I planned on a divorce, but I thought a fresh start in a new country would be good for us all."

Helen was now furious. "Then you thought wrong, husband. Do what you will, but if you are going to leave with another woman, I am certainly not coming with you. I don't know how you could behave in this manner. It is disgraceful and shameful that you could lead me along and then tell me this at the last moment. You are a coward and a cheat. Go to Harvard. Go to your woman and good luck. Leave my passport, but I doubt I shall ever use it. Listen, there is the taxi. Go. Just go."

Percival spluttered. "This house went with my job – what will you do?"

"It is apparent you have no concern for your family. Goodness knows what the two older boys will think. It seems as if you have severed yourself from us. Well, so be it. There is the taxi – Go!"

Percival took one look at his wife's face. Catherine and Stuart just stood frozen to the spot. All they really understood was their mother's distress and the fact that their father seemed to be leaving without them.

Percival just turned on his heel and walked out of the door. Empty rooms seemed to echo as he banged the door.

"What are we going to do, Mum?" asked Stuart.

"I don't know, son, I just don't know."

Helen sat down on one of the boxes that remained and sobbed.

Catherine began to cry. Stuart, at thirteen, felt the responsibility on his shoulders.

"We can't stay here, Mum, can we?" he ventured.

Helen pulled herself together. She loved all her children, but in her heart Stuart, her youngest boy, had always been her favourite. He seemed so bright and so knowing, but this blow had been totally unforeseen even for him. She realised that she must stay strong for the children.

"We don't really need to leave here for another week," she volunteered. "We still have the key as a neighbour was going to drop it into the college for us after we left. We can stay here tonight."

"Where will we sleep?" worried Catherine.

"Where we usually do. They weren't going to take the beds as we were going to buy new in America," answered Helen. "There are the bunk beds and one four-foot and one single still here. There are a lot of boxes here as you know your father had packed his things in a trunk and his boxes have gone."

Stuart began to poke the boxes. "This one's soft, Mum," he detected.

They opened the box and indeed there were the sheets, pillow cases and blankets. Helen soon put these on the beds.

"We've got nothing to eat or drink," complained Catherine.

Helen buried her pride and went to her next-door neighbour. She just simply explained that she felt that she could not go to America.

The neighbour, Mrs Banks, was sympathetic. "It's a big thing to up and move. Can I help?"

"I'm afraid we're not sure what is in the boxes. I would be grateful if you could let us have some milk, tea, biscuits and lend us a kettle."

"That is no problem," exclaimed Mrs Banks. "I do have two electric kettles. Is the power still on?"

"Oh yes. The house is not finally returned to the college for another week. I expect another family will take it over eventually."

Mrs Banks decided to say nothing, but she understood Helen's predicament. She quickly got some tea, sugar and milk together, plus a kettle and helped to take it into the house. She did gasp when she saw so many boxes. She piped up, "Are these being collected?" she asked tentatively.

"They were," replied Helen, "but I shall keep them now until I know where we are going."

Mrs Banks again tactfully said no more.

Helen and the children had tea and biscuits and although it was early, they retreated to bed.

Chapter 4

The next day, Helen took money from the safe and packed a bag and they walked to the council offices. It was a long walk. There were ushered to the right department and a sympathetic council worker heard their predicament.

"We can put you in temporary accommodation for today if you wish," she volunteered. "An evening meal and breakfast will be provided."

"We have our beds at home," Catherine piped up.

"But have you food?" enquired the council worker, named Sadie.

Catherine was silent. They had eaten Mrs Banks' biscuits. An evening meal sounded inviting.

"Fortunately," said Sadie, "there is a flat becoming available tomorrow. You have a precedence as you have two children. Here is the address. It seemed close to the schools the children attended. Here is a key, but you can't use it until tomorrow. Luckily, we have a spare key. Now do go to the temporary accommodation, 'The Baines Crest House' now."

"But what about our boxes and things still left at our house?" enquired Helen. "The beds are still there as well. The packers can't get in to take them as we locked all the doors, but we shall need things for the new flat."

"Don't worry," Sadie stated. "Give me your key and we will send removal men to take everything to the flat. It will be free by 11am tomorrow. I will try to arrange for the removal men to have your things by 11am. Who are the packers?"

"Robertson and Robertson," answered Helen. "They were going to take the remaining items to the store for shipment."

"Don't worry," added Sadie, "we will contact them and cancel. Go to the Baines Crest House, have a good meal and try to sleep. It is a good place and they have helped us many times."

Helen thanked Sadie and turned away. She had her small bag with her because some instinct made her unsure of the council's response. She had also emptied the small safe before she left. Percival had made no mention of money when she refused to leave and seemed to have forgotten about the safe. There was little in it in any case. The rental agreement was with the college, but there was fifty pounds in notes.

Helen turned back to Sadie. "Most of the furniture has been packed and already sent for shipment," she said. "There are the beds as I said, because my husband wanted new ones, and several rugs have been left, but what do we do for the rest of the furniture?"

"I'm afraid the last tenant of the flat was evicted," said Sadie. "We were going to clear the flat as the previous tenant has gone home to her mother; there are curtains, tables, chairs, settees and even a television. The tenant did not want to bother with anything when she left.

"If you wish to purchase new items, we can remove the ones there."

"Oh no!" exclaimed Helen. "We shall be grateful for anything there, at least for the time being. I'm sorry but I can't really think straight at the moment. I am still in shock that this has all happened."

"Just take a step at a time, my dear." Sadie smiled. "Gosh, look at the time, it is my finishing time. I have a four-seater car in the car park. Come, I will drop you off at the guest house."

Sadie quickly tidied her desk, then spoke to a colleague. "My colleague will ring Robertson and Robertson to cancel the packing being sent to the ship's terminal and arrange for everything left in the house to be brought to the flat. If there is anything in the flat you do not require, just leave it outside the main door and we will get it collected."

Sadie turned and they all left. Sadie took them to her car and true to her word left them at the guest house.

The proprietress was kindly when they arrived. She showed them to their room, a double and a single bed, and told them the time of the evening meal.

Helen sat on the bed, still stunned. She was fond of the house they had lived in for years, but everything had suddenly turned upside down. She still couldn't believe that Percival could just turn his back on his family. She knew that such things happened to other people, but didn't think it would happen to her. She mused again, how cowardly of him to leave it until the last moment to apprise her of the situation. Any love she had felt for him died.

Catherine and Stuart had been mostly silent, knowing that something dreadful had happened to their family, but not quite sure what it all entailed. They accepted that they certainly weren't going on a big adventure to America, but they too didn't really want to lose their home or leave their friends. It was the life they knew that seemed to be falling apart. They had said goodbye to their friends at their schools and of course the schools had been notified of their departure.

"I suggest we go round to Catherine's school and explain that we are no longer leaving England. The new flat's address is only a bus ride away."

Helen didn't tell the children that the flat was in what was called a 'downmarket' area. It actually had a bad reputation and the area was known as 'The Bronx', which was probably unfair as in America The Bronx is ranked dead last in the annual health report by the University of Wisconsin and the Robert Wood Johnson Foundation which ranked the 62 New York counties. It is also known for its high crime rate and is home to some of the most dangerous neighbourhoods in New York City including Hunts Point and Mott Haven. The area contains the poorest congressional district in the USA.

Helen felt that the nickname was unjust and unfair, but the flat was available and where else could she go or even afford to go?

Chapter 5

Helen and the children went to Catherine's school. The headmistress was still there although time had passed. Helen explained simply that they were no longer going to America and gave the new address which had been given to her. She explained that they were moving to the new address the next day and could Catherine return to her old class the following Monday? Helen left out details because she was still traumatised with the whole situation and did not wish for further discussions. The Headmistress was perceptive and realised that something traumatic must have occurred, but stated simply that she would be pleased for her to return, and she would be reinstated on the register. They then took a bus to Stuart's school and gave the same explanation.

The family returned to the guest house, had their meal and again they had an early night.

Helen could not sleep. She kept going over events again and again. Percival had come home most evenings, and they had all eaten together as a family. When had he been able to start a love affair with the bursar? She remembered now that he had said he had to attend a seminar in Cambridge, but that was only for four days. Had those four days been the stepping stones to this debacle? Perhaps they had managed to get to a hotel in his free periods at the college. Their own love making had always been mutually satisfying, but Helen now realised that it had recently been very infrequent. Percival had, however, still been civil and kindly to the children. He had a personal bank account, but always gave her a generous allowance each month for clothes and housekeeping. He had paid all the bills, electric, gas, water, telephone and council tax, so she had had no financial worries.

"What will happen now?" she pondered to herself. She would get the family allowance but that was meagre. She had heard from friends that when receiving National Assistance, the rent would be paid, but what about utility bills? Helen at last fell into a troubled sleep.

The next day after a very nice breakfast at the boarding house, they collected the few things they had. Helen held on tightly to the money she had, and they went to the Co-op and got some groceries.

At 11am they went to the flat. Fortunately, it was a ground floor flat, with a very small piece of allotted garden. They opened the door with the key tentatively. It smelled a bit musty but it was tidy. There was a three-piece suite in the sitting room, with an open fireplace. The dining room was in Ercol style. The carpets were a dull green. The kitchen was very basic: an oven, sink, table and chairs and a small refrigerator. There were, however, inset cupboards in the kitchen. The bedrooms were bare, there were two, and Helen hoped the removal men would soon bring their beds. There were, however, also inset cupboards in the bedrooms.

The bathroom was in black and white with the toilet in the bathroom.

Helen sighed. At least it was habitable. At that moment the removal men arrived with the beds, and also brought the boxes not taken by the packers. Helen knew that one box would contain the bed linen, but she couldn't remember what the other boxes contained. Some were labelled, however, and fortunately much kitchenware was there, bathroom lights, some mirrors, pictures and their clothes. The removal men brought the bed covers and linen.

"Will Dad send us any money?" asked Stuart, bright as usual.

"I don't know," retorted Helen. "I am afraid it may be unlikely. He seems to have abandoned us completely. We have a little money but I want to keep that mainly for any emergency. Now, let's unpack the boxes. Look, Stuart, the previous tenant has left hooks in the wall. You can put pictures and mirrors on them where you think best. I will sort out the kitchen equipment."

"What shall I do?" asked Catherine.

"Here is the box with the bed linen," replied Helen. "Do you think you could make up the beds?"

"I'll try," replied Catherine.

Eventually the flat was sorted and Helen left the children to their own devices. Fortunately, one box contained books that the children read and test books for Stuart. Another contained some toys including a Meccano set, a teddy bear and some dolls.

Helen went to the local shops using a little of the money she had found in the safe. She bought simple food, cereals for breakfast, milk, tea, sugar, fishfingers and peas. She also bought some soup. She realised that she had to be very frugal.

When she returned, Stuart had done a good job in the placing of mirrors and pictures, and Catherine had made up the bunk beds and the four foot bed quite well. Stuart had found an electric fire which he had put in the fireplace, but Helen was worried about the running cost. The flat did have central heating with a gas boiler. At least they had a home.

Chapter 6

The children returned to their schools. They had been given bus passes by the Council and had found their uniforms in the boxes. To his joy Stuart was now put into the fourteen-year-old group. He was indeed exceptionally bright. He had known for a long time all the main capital cities in the world, the rivers and deserts. He was quick at languages, mathematics and science, and his English vocabulary was exceptional. Catherine was happy to be back in her class. Helen, however, was not so fortunate. When she contacted her previous friends, she was met with total hostility. As the wife of a lecturer it appeared she was respected and worthy of their friendship, but now that the news had quickly spread that she was living in 'The Bronx' in council property and had been deserted apparently by her husband, the friends that she thought she had no longer wished to be associated with her. Only Mrs Bunds, an old neighbour, was still friendly, but Helen realised that now she had to battle alone as a single parent with two children. She had not been able to contact her two older children and it would be difficult to accommodate her sons when they did know of the move.

She visited the Council offices again and found out how much her allowance would be, which seemed horribly small upon which to live. She could not purchase any new items as she had so little money.

She bought the cheapest food, but suddenly there was a gas bill for £85 which the previous tenant had not paid. Helen appealed against this, but the previous tenant had now moved away completely with a new man, according to gossip. She could not be located and the gas board were hounding Helen. She appealed to the Council, but even they no longer appeared helpful. Sadie had moved to another position and Helen felt desperate.

Stuart was very aware of his mother's problems. He went to the local baker and asked if he needed help.

"I do," replied Mr Birch. "But you are only a lad. I can't employ you."

"I am tall for my age," answered Stuart. He lied and said, "I am 14. If you give me cash no one will know my age. They may think I'm your son. I can easily deliver if you give me some addresses and I will knock and get more customers."

Mr Birch fell for the boy's intelligence and good looks. Indeed, Stuart did look fourteen. He had black curly hair, sparkling eyes full of intelligence and a wonderful smile.

"Ok. I just hope I don't run into any trouble, but you are certainly tall for your age. But what about your schooling?"

"I can do 7.30am until 8.30am in the week and I can do one hour after school in the evening, but then I must do my homework or study. I can work all day Saturday."

"Fine," said Mr Birch. "I will give you £1.10s a week. You can help me in the shop and do a few deliveries if necessary on Saturday. Start next Monday." Mr Birch was a kindly soul and he handed Stuart a pound note.

"Here, lad, take this as a golden handshake." Mr Birch did not ask the boy whey he needed the money but could see that the lad looked pale and worried. He guessed of course that there was a family problem rather than the boy wanting to buy a treat for himself.

Chapter 7

Helen was glad of the extra money that Stuart brought in. With the family allowance and Stuart's money she managed to scrape by for a month, but they often went hungry and could not buy anything new. A further blow enfolded when a divorce document was served upon her from America. It seemed that Percival had somehow managed to get a 'quick' divorce and there was no mention of any financial reparation He had just cut himself off completely from his family and when Helen recovered from the shock, she told her children.

Catherine didn't really understand, but Stuart felt very bitter. He had not really been close to his father, who always seemed so absorbed in his work, but they had been a family. Now he felt cut adrift and it made him feel very bitter. He felt that now he had no father and felt more than ever the responsibility of being 'the man' of the house.

Helen tried to contact her other two sons and tell them of events, but when they did get the information, it seemed as if they were determined to maintain their own lifestyles and they seemed to have no wish to return home. News from them became very sparse. They knew about 'The Bronx' and it appeared that they made no effort to return to their new home. Helen and Stuart picked up on their response to all that had happened and of course Helen loved her sons. She just felt confused, but again his brothers' attitude reinforced the bitterness that was building up inside Stuart.

Although now in the class with fourteen year olds, Stuart's school work began to suffer. He became friendly with a group of boys from the council estate and some of them bragged about what they had managed to steal. This influenced Stuart.

He did not steal from Mr Birch, but several times took items from a supermarket without paying. He managed to take items that his mother and sister could eat, such as baked beans, spaghetti hoops and fish fingers. He went in with his school bag and managed to shove them inside. Amazingly, he did not get caught.

He felt so bitter that he had no compunction for his actions. He felt that life had dealt his mother and sister a bitter blow and that what he did was only some kind of retaliation.

He felt also that he was entitled to some fun. He felt it quite wrong that he should be embroiled with all the misery that seemed to now surround his life.

When one of his new friends suggested looking for cars on drives, still with the key in the ignition, he went along with this.

When his mother and Catherine were asleep, he would steal out with his new friends, find a car, and they would drive for miles and then return it to the drive from whence it came. This became a usual nightly game. One of the older boys had learned to drive and Stuart soon picked it up. They became more adventurous and actually drove to London one night in the 'borrowed' car. Again, miraculously, they were not discovered.

Time went by. Stuart still worked for Mr Birch, but with his nightly adventures was often too tired to do well at school. He could have sat examinations at sixteen, but he realised that he was not studying sufficiently and would probably fail. He was also losing interest in his schooling.

Helen fortunately managed to get a position at a checkout in a local supermarket. This was a great boost and enabled them to have discount food stuffs. Stuart no longer had the need to steal, but still went out some nights with his new friends who managed to find cigarettes and alcohol. Stuart began to think that this was great fun, and decided that he was definitely tired of all the sadness that had befallen his mother and the family.

Chapter 8

Helen became friendly with a stacker at the store. He was a widower whose first wife had died of cancer. Helen had dark brown curly hair, a good figure and a kindly nature. The shelf stacker would talk to her at tea breaks and invited her to his flat for coffee in the lunch break. This could only happen in the week, because of the children. Her hours were tailored, starting at nine and finishing at three, as she had to pick Catherine up from school. However, the friendship with the shelf stacker developed. Helen told him of her husband's desertion and that now he had finally divorced her. The shelf stacker's name was Simon, and very quickly asked Helen to marry him. Helen was unsure of this because of the children. She invited him to the flat to meet Catherine and Stuart. Stuart liked the guy and felt that this friendship between Simon and his mother could be a boon and finally take the responsibility from his shoulders. Very quickly Simon moved into their flat – his own had only been rented. Some of his furniture, however, was of higher quality than the furniture Helen had inherited from the previous occupant of her flat. Simon hired a van and his furniture was installed. He arranged for Helen's inherited furniture to go to a charity shop.

They registered for a registry office wedding in Portsmouth.

Catherine was pleased that Simon became part of their household and called him Daddy very quickly. Simon was an easy-going man, and kind to both children. He took on evening work at the supermarket to boost finances and life became much happier for the family. Helen was able to buy new clothes for herself and better clothes and shoes for the children.

Stuart had a new blazer, rather than one of his elder brother's hand-me-downs. Catherine had new dresses and Helen was able to afford new outfits for herself. Stuart liked Simon and also respected him for the great affection he extended to his mother. He stopped his nightly excursions with his friends and if Simon was not too tired after ostensibly doing two jobs, would play cards with him and Simon taught him to play chess.

Simon and Helen married privately, with just two witnesses and Catherine and Stuart present.

Stuart was still working for Mr Birch but still not doing too well now at school. Stuart eventually turned fifteen but, strangely, his birthday passed unnoticed. This was because Helen was excited because she was pregnant and had told the children that they were going to have a new baby brother or sister. Helen had only been eighteen when she married

Percival. Her older sons were twenty and twenty-one and Helen was now thirty-nine. When Stuart heard the news he was not pleased. He felt that a new baby would once again unsettle the newfound family contentment. Even he had started to call Simon 'dad'. Catherine seemed unbothered and probably thought the new baby would be like a new doll with which to play. Stuart found out where the army recruitment officers were and decided to become an army cadet. Helen understood her son and gave her permission. This meant that Stuart would leave home and go to the army cadet training centre in Carlisle. He would receive a small salary and training in multiple skills such as general military skills, preparations for extended field operations and leading participating and conducting small unit tactical operations, plus two short courses in First Aid and basic shooting. This led to the Army Proficiency Certificate. After completion Stuart could join the army with parental consent.

Chapter 9

S tuart left home with some regret, but had begun to feel an 'outsider' in his home. Much as he admired Simon for his endeavours and love of his mother, he felt 'left out'. Now with a new baby on the horizon, he felt pushed back even further. He felt that he really must get on with his own life, although of course he loved his mother dearly. He also felt that he had outgrown his friends from 'The Bronx'. They were not up to his intellectual level and he had begun to feel their pranks and antics puerile. He was sorry to say goodbye to Mr Birch and felt indebted to him for his kindness, but he felt that he must move on with his life and felt the army offered more scope and excitement.

He certainly didn't want to be involved with all that was entailed with a newborn baby. Helen loved her son, but she too was now so involved with her new husband and the new life that was within her.

Stuart made brief farewells, to make parting less painful, and was given transport to Carlisle. From being a student, to 'man of the house', then daredevil with his friends, it was rather a rude culture shock to be in a regimented organisation, but he gritted his teeth, determined to make a success of this opportunity. Deep down he still felt a bitterness at the desertion of his father, and secretly thought that if this had not occurred, he may well have been secure and passed his school examinations, and entered a university. He thought he may well have read history or geography. But that was now in the past. He had a new life as an army cadet, and probably in the army, and must succeed.

Stuart did not make friends easily as an army cadet. He was known to be short tempered and tended to feel superior in intellect to his fellow cadets. He managed to endure the regimentation with difficulty, but excelled at all the courses provided. When it came to the final Army Proficiency Certificate, he passed with flying colours and immediately enrolled in the army. He was sent to the Middle East and then back to Holland where he met a lovely Dutch girl in a bar. He was occasionally able to stay at her parents' house when on leave from duties, and for the first time experienced the joys of sexual gratification. Monica fell in love with this handsome young man, and although now only just nineteen, Stuart bought her an engagement ring. It was quite simple, a small opal on a gold band, but Monica was delighted and her parents continued to allow him to sleep over when possible in their house.

Stuart very much enjoyed sex, and Monica was a willing partner. The trouble was that her parents began to talk of marriage and Monica began to talk of having a baby.

Stuart seemed to be leading two lives. One at his army barracks, doing field work, and a great deal of shooting practice, and now being coaxed by Monica and her parents into marriage. Stuart had not been home now for some considerable time and when he had returned it was only on brief visits. Helen had given birth to a son, and Stuart was not interested in his new half-brother. His sister, however, seemed happy to still be at home. The thought of having a baby with Monica filled him with horror and, even worse, Monica's parents seemed to have arranged a wedding without his consent. Stuart was incensed and arranged with his superior at the army barracks to have a transfer. He told Monica that he could no longer be engaged, he certainly didn't wish to wed, and definitely did not want a baby. Monica cried so loudly that her parents came into the room. Upon hearing the reason for this debacle, Monica's father told him to get out. Stuart left hastily with a muttered apology and Monica threw the little opal ring at him as he left. It just fell unnoticed to the floor. Stuart felt that he had had a lucky escape as he had felt a net closing in around him. He returned to his barracks, and was soon sent back to the Middle East where the problems were severe in Oman.

Chapter 10

The problem was the rebellion against the Sultan and there was a rebellion called the Dhofar Rebellion. Britain assisted the Omani Government by sending soldiers. In 1970, the Sultan of Oman Said bin Taimur was overthrown by his son Qaboos bin Said. The Rebellion had been happening since 1963, but the coup d'état of overthrowing the Sultan Omar Said bin Talmur was on 23rd July 1970. Guerillas known as the Adoo were Communists and targeting the Omani Government. The United Kingdom were sending aid and had a military base located with the Al Duqm Port and Drydock of Duqm in the Al Wusta Governorate of Oman. Soldiers operated alongside the Royal Army of Oman. The guerrillas were finally defeated at the Battle of Mirbat on 19th July 1972.

Stuart was involved in all this mayhem but not in the front line. He had to learn to obey on command in a life and death situation. Throughout his life he had found obeying orders difficult. He had survived in the Cadets, but in Oman as the war heated up, there was no choice but to obey commands. However, he managed and on the conclusion of the war was promoted to Lance Corporal. He did not revisit his home at all during this time. He felt that he wanted to flap his wings, and shake the dust off the Council Estate from his feet.

As Lance Corporal, he was sent to Belize which had a challenging terrain. British soldiers were given world class training in how to survive, live and fight in the jungle. Stuart was now getting bored with this life. His new posting was to be in Germany and after a great deal of thought whilst still in Belize, at 25, he decided to leave the army. No one could persuade him to stay, and he went home.

Catherine was now nineteen and had taken on work as a receptionist at a doctor's surgery. She was going out with a young man called Malcolm. Helen had given birth again to a brother Stuart had hitherto not seen. Simon was working hard and Helen was of course delighted to see Stuart. His older brothers seemed to have totally deserted the family as had Stuart for a long while. He did not feel comfortable in the home. He liked Simon, but felt little for his two new brothers. He loved his mother, but she was totally involved with his new brothers, concerned with their education and hobbies.

He decided to take a flat in Portsmouth. He still had savings from the army and now a small pension.

He looked around and found a cheap studio flat that he felt would serve him well.

His mother, understanding his need for independence, wished him well.

Stuart visited some charity shops and purchased some second-hand furniture, a bed, table, chairs, etc, and items for cooking. He felt suddenly rather alone. He had always been surrounded by people, so began to visit the local public houses. Here he was introduced to cannabis. He bought some weed, smoked it and enjoyed it. He began to drink heavily. In one public house called the 'Cock and Bull', he met a pretty blonde girl called Charmaine. He bought her a drink and she told him that she had just fallen out with her boyfriend. Stuart provided a shoulder for her to cry on and invited her round to his flat. She readily agreed, and they soon ended up in his bed. Stuart had had a long time of abstinence from sex, and was delighted to find such a willing partner. They both caressed, kissed and over the night Stuart thought they both had at least three orgasms.

Chapter 11

Charmaine was 25 and was a shop assistant. She had a small flat of her own, but was spending most nights at Stuart's studio flat. They spent the evenings drinking and having sex. But once again, Stuart began to feel rather trapped. He hadn't decided what to do with his life, and lovely as Charmaine was, he certainly did not want to settle down in marriage. To his dismay one evening Charmaine stated that she thought she was pregnant. Stuart looked so horrified, that Charmaine began to cry.

"You must marry me," she said.

Stuart replied, "I have no job as yet, just a small army pension and a little saved. I thought you were on the pill."

"I forgot to take it," cried Charmaine.

"I don't believe you. One forgotten pill is unlikely to cause pregnancy."

"What are you going to do?"

"I don't know. I am sorry but I am not prepared for a permanent relationship at present, nor do I want a child. My own father abandoned us and I'm afraid that I may turn out like him. I also know the hardships we endured when he did. I would not wish that on anyone."

Charmaine left the flat in tears but returned the next evening saying that she was mistaken and there was no baby.

Stuart felt that the whole situation had been to trap him into a permanent relationship.

"I have enjoyed your company, Charmaine," he said, "but I am afraid it has to end."

Without another word he left Charmaine in the studio flat and went to the 'Cock and Bull' where he found some weed and got thoroughly drunk. When he went home Charmaine had gone but had left a note.

'Stuart, you can be very charming and we have had a great time, but I think your background has warped you. You only seem to think about yourself and that is not a good thing. However, I wish you well. Charmaine.'

Stuart read the note, tore it up and put the pieces in the bin. "So be it," he thought. "I'm nobody's fool and not going to be pushed around."

Chapter 12

Stuart was relieved to have escaped the clutches of Charmaine but had to admit to himself that the sex had been great. She had been such a willing participant in some of his fantasies, but he had no wish to marry. He had seen what his mother had suffered and was secretly afraid that some of his father's traits could be in his DNA. He wasn't sure that he could be faithful to one woman; in fact, he didn't think he wanted to be monogamous. It seemed more fun to explore sex with different women, and he felt that he would eventually get bored with just one partner. His worry at the present, however, was finance. As stated, his army pension was small, and he had already spent most of his savings. He was spending a lot on drink, some weed and cigarettes. He had to earn some money, but how? His stepfather had done some work on the railway, and he decided to apply for this as a temporary option. He was accepted, but the hours were unsocial.

He was a quick learner and soon learned how to repair and instal rail track, but it was dangerous and often meant working at the weekend. When possible, he still went to public houses drinking and met a young lady named Yvonne, who seemed fun. She was single and fancy-free as it were. She was a few years older than he and already had had several failed relationships. He enticed her to his studio flat and listened to all her tales of woe. She was an attractive girl, however, with a good bust and long legs. She also had long blonde hair which he liked. She seemed avid for sex, but Stuart was now cautious. He made sure that he always wore a condom. He felt that this distracted from his sexual pleasure, but he was not going to get trapped by a pregnancy. Yvonne was feisty and good company. She was a good drinking partner and her hours as a hairdresser enabled her to come to his flat when he was free. She lived with her mother nearby, so did not have far to travel.

As an attractive man he had no problem in finding women. One night he went to the pub on his own. Yvonne was visiting her sister. He caught the eye of a dark haired girl and smiled at her. She came over almost at once. He bought her a gin and tonic and chatted her up. She, too, like Yvonne, had had several failed relationships. She was quite overt and said to him, "Would you like to have sex with me? I could come round to your place, wherever it is."

Stuart thought frantically. Yvonne now had a key to his studio flat and could come back at any time. This girl hadn't offered her premises. For all he knew she could actually be living with someone. He certainly didn't want any trouble.

"Well," she said. "How about it?"

"No, thank you," Stuart replied. Wondering if perhaps they could just have a quickie outside.

"Do you usually turn girls down?" the girl enquired, obviously feeling misread.

Stuart decided to be brutally honest. "No!" he said, looking her in the eye.

The girl was incensed. She brought her hand up and slapped Stuart across the face, turned and left. There were several people in the pub who witnessed this scene. Stuart wondered if they thought that he had made some unwanted sexual advance. He knew the slap was deserved, but still felt embarrassed.

He decided to go back to his studio flat. To his amazement Yvonne was there, but she was looking into one of his drawers in a little cabinet and some of his post was on her lap.

"What are you doing?" he said, rather angrily.

"Reading some of your post. I want to know a lot more about you."

Stuart was furious. The post was fairly mundane, details of his small army pension and a bank statement or two, but again he felt a net closing around him with this invasion of his privacy.

"I want you to leave," he said. "Please leave my flat key as you go."

"Are you serious, you don't want to see me again?"

"Deadly serious," retorted Stuart. "You have overstepped the mark. I wouldn't dream of looking at your correspondence."

"I am sorry, can't we forget it?" cajoled Yvonne.

"No. We have had mutual fun, but I can't trust you anymore. Please leave."

Yvonne took the key from her purse and threw it at him.

"What is wrong with you?" she shouted. "Just looking at a bit of old post isn't a crime. I was just passing the time until you returned. Who are you to be so judgemental? You are just a nobody. This flat is poky and all you do is work on a railway. I want someone with a nice car and good salary."

"I didn't see you refusing sex."

"Well women have needs as well. But I don't need someone with a temper. Goodbye."

Yvonne went out and slammed the door as she left.

Well, that is that, thought Stuart. But it made him reflect on his work. He wasn't particularly well paid and he didn't have a car. He had driven several vehicles in the army from necessity, but he hadn't invested in a car or obtained a licence.

He decided that he would obtain a driving licence and then change his job. He went to sleep that night in a very thoughtful mood.

Chapter 13

The next day Stuart went to the Driving Test Centre and booked a test. (He had his documents with him from his driving in the army.) It was, to him, a large amount of money to invest, but he considered it worth it.

He then went to his boss at the railway and told him he was leaving. He asked for his wages to be put in the bank but forfeited some due to not giving a month's notice. He then went to a local garage and for £300 bought a blue second-hand van which he considered more practical for his needs.

He shouldn't have driven it, but he bluffed his way through and drove it to a parking area outside his flat. This was free for residents.

He thought he would hedge his bets and wait to insure the vehicle and pay road tax when he had passed his test.

"So far, so good," he thought. He then had to decide on work. He had some cash left and went to the local public house again. Making a few discreet enquiries he was able to purchase some cannabis. Moving on to another public house he was then able to sell this. This way of making money seemed much easier than working on the railway. However, he knew that he must do something else. Luck was on his side. One of his acquaintances in the public house The Swan, needed a house sitter. The friend was going away for a month and had two dogs. When Stuart heard this, he offered his services immediately. His offer was accepted for quite a large sum of money, £400.

Stuart was soon ensconced in a large detached house, a large garden (which apparently had a gardener) with two King Charles Cavaliers. He had come across dogs in the army, but these were two very spoilt Blenheim coloured dogs. He had had instructions on food and all he had to do was to keep the place tidy and walk the dogs. This suited him admirably. He took the dogs to various public houses and did a bit of wheeling and dealing and in one public house a dark haired girl was sitting on her own and it looked as if she had been crying.

Stuart seized the opportunity and went over to her.

"May I help?" he enquired.

"I share my flat with my boyfriend and he has just walked out. I am a nurse and can still afford the rent on the flat, but I feel discarded and embarrassed."

"Why did he leave?" asked Stuart.

"We quarrelled. I think he has met someone else but I don't really know. We haven't been together very long and he just moved into my flat."

Stuart bought her a vodka and lime and they continued to talk.

"Come back to my place," offered Stuart. "I have only come out to give the dogs a walk."

"Oh, what are their names?"

Luckily Stuart knew this. "Brandon and Bijon," he said.

"Oh, they are lovely. May I pat them?"

"I don't know your name."

"Isobelle."

"Well my name is Stuart. Come home with me just for company. Forget your bloke, my house has several bedrooms – you will be quite safe. I can make you a cappuccino and at least you won't be alone."

Isobelle looked at the handsome young man and thought, "If he is good to dogs, that is a good sign."

Smiling, she accepted.

"Thank you so much," she said. "I feel quite shattered."

When Stuart got back to the house he was house sitting, Isobelle was most impressed.

"It is a lovely place," she said. "How on earth did you afford it?"

"Oh, I do some business deals," replied Stuart airily. He showed her into the main sitting room, which had a long table with twelve chairs, a lovely Chinese rug and some excellent side tables. Stuart had wondered how his acquaintance could afford a house, but apparently his mate's parents had died, he was the only son, and it was inherited.

Isobelle was quite overcome. Stuart made her a cappuccino and then showed her to one of the four bedrooms, but not the one that he was using.

"I could sleep with you," volunteered Isobelle, "but could we just cuddle?"

"Certainly," replied Stuart. "Get under the covers whilst I see to the dogs."

Brandon and Bijon had been fed and their beds were in the kitchen. Stuart shut the door and went upstairs.

Isobelle was under the covers in just her bra and pants. Stuart undressed and slid in beside her. He put his arm round her and asked if she was alright.

"I'm fine," she said. "It's so lovely here. You are so lucky."

Stuart smiled to himself and said nothing. He felt that he should indeed have a house like this and cursed his father again mentally for deserting them and leaving the family to fend for themselves. He guessed that his father would be earning a large salary in America, but none of it had come their way.

Isobelle fell asleep and before long it seemed that morning had come. It was time to feed the dogs, and what was he going to do about Isobelle?

Luckily, she solved the problem. "I have to be at work at nine," she said. "It isn't far from here. I can walk."

"Let me make you toast and coffee," volunteered Stuart, which he did.

"Shall I come back this evening?" asked Isobelle hopefully. "It would be lovely to walk in the garden. I expect my boyfriend has taken his things from my flat and I don't want to be alone."

"Well shall we say you come about seven," said Stuart. "It is still light then. I have so enjoyed your company. Thank you for coming back with me last night."

Giving her a light kiss on the cheek, Stuart showed her out.

"Gosh!" he thought. "What have I got myself into."

He fed and walked the dogs and got himself a beef burger from a kiosk. He went back to the house and decided to watch the television. He was able to do a bit of wheeling and dealing in the afternoon and was back at the house when Isobelle came.

That night Isobelle made it clear that she would welcome any sexual advances. She was not a virgin, and Stuart felt no conscience about this. Although she said that she was on the pill, Stuart took no chances and always wore a condom. The sex was satisfying but not particularly exciting. She was of slight stature and had small breasts. Stuart actually preferred a large bust, but she was available, and Stuart found her intelligent company. She did return to her own place briefly but now began to spend every night with Stuart. He was able to afford to either buy food, which mainly could be microwaved, or he took her to inexpensive restaurants or for pub meals. He made sure that the dogs were well cared for, he was careful about the house and the gardener did not know that Isobelle existed due to his hours.

Amazingly, Stuart was given an early date for his driving test due to a cancellation. Saying nothing, he took it and passed. He didn't think Isobelle would be impressed with his blue van, which he could now drive, but then he could say it was just for his business.

He was beginning to get used to Isobelle coming to the house. He felt happier than he had for a long time. His drug dealing was gathering momentum and he had to admit that sex with Isobelle was satisfying. She did query why he wore a condom, when she was on the pill, but Stuart was at least honest about this.

"I have no wish to be a father," he explained.

Isobelle felt it was a touchy subject, so wisely said nothing. She felt, however, that she had found a handsome young man, they were sexually compatible and she just loved the house, gardens and even the dogs. She felt hopeful that this could be a permanent relationship and that maybe his antipathy to fatherhood would eventually go.

Stuart was in cloud cuckoo land. He almost began to believe that this life was for him. Of course, he didn't consider that bills that had to be paid, to the current gardener (which had been paid in advance) or the utilities. He was a Walter Mitty. He had paid the insurance for his van and the road tax. Isobelle accepted that this van was purely for his work when he drove it to the house, parking it on the drive.

They were fast asleep in bed, after having had a passionate sexual night. There was a loud bang, a lot of barking and a voice called.

"Hey mate, I'm home. Sorry it's so late, but the plane was delayed."

Stuart sat up horrified as the door burst open. Isobelle sat up looking frightened, as the owner entered.

"What's happening," she cried. "Who are you? Stuart, what is it?"

"I'm Barry, my dear and I live here."

"Do you share this house with Stuart?"

"This is my house, my dear. I don't blame Stuart for having company, but from tomorrow I want my house to myself. I'm sure Stuart has done a good job, but here I am now."

"I don't understand," said Isobelle. "I thought this was Stuart's house."

"No, my dear, he has been house sitting for me, to look after my two dogs. I have been away on a business trip to Holland."

Isobelle could not take this in. "Stuart, is this true?"

Stuart felt dreadful. His dream world had crashed around him. He just said curtly, "Yes!"

"Well, where do you really live?"

Stuart gave her the address of his studio flat.

"This is just a hiccup," he blustered. "It doesn't need to affect our relationship. You can come to my studio flat."

Isobelle got up and got dressed.

"I really believed that this was your house," she cried. "You let me think that it was. You talked about it as if it was yours. I really began to believe that we may live here as partners one day. You have been cruel to deceive me." Isobelle was crying.

Barry intervened. "I think, my dear, that you have been conned. Sadly this has gone to Stuart's head. I think that you had both better leave now."

Despite the fact that it was only four in the morning Stuart and Isobelle got dressed. Neither spoke to the other until Stuart said, "Isobelle, you come home with me to my flat. I'll drive you in the van."

"No, thank you," replied Isobelle. She felt that all her dreams were shattered. "I shall walk and go back to my own flat."

"Let me drive you," begged Stuart hopefully. "I can stay at your place."

"No! This has all been such a shock, I need to be alone."

Stuart gathered up his few things and Barry watched silently.

The pair left by the front door but went their separate ways. Isobelle walked one way and Stuart drove back to his flat.

When Stuart went into his studio flat, it did seem so small. He had so enjoyed the grandeur of the large house. All his bitterness about his life resurged.

"Why do some people have all the luck," he mused. "Who says that they are more deserving than me?"

He wallowed in self-pity and could not sleep. Somehow, he still felt that his chequered life was all mainly due to his father's desertion. This thread kept recurring in his mind. He began to feel ill and realised that he needed to pull himself together. Isobelle shouldn't have got used to the idea that the large house was not his. She could have fallen in love with him sufficiently to gloss over the change of circumstances. He knew that he wasn't in love with her, but he had got used to her and used to regular sex. He realised that he didn't actually know where she lived. He could track her through the hospital where she was a nurse, he thought. But would they release her address? The more he thought about it the more confused he became. He smoked some weed to calm himself.

"I shall just have to see if she contacts me," he thought and finally managed to sleep.

Chapter 14

He heard nothing from Isobelle and had to concentrate on finding work.

He temporarily took a job stacking shelves in a supermarket. The money was not good, but he did manage to get food cheaply that was out of date.

One day, as he was restacking the shelves, a young woman with little in her basket asked if he knew where the sugar was located. She was small and pretty with fair curly hair. He guessed she was in her early twenties.

"I shouldn't have sugar," she offered. "But I do indulge now and again."

"Me too," stated Stuart. "Mainly, however, I have cappuccino which doesn't need sugar."

"Oh, I love cappuccino," retorted the young woman.

Stuart decided to be bold. "Do you have a boyfriend or partner?"

"No, I have given up for the time being. My last boyfriend was too controlling."

"Would you have a coffee with me?"

"When would that be? I'm working in a nail parlour at the moment and don't finish until five."

"Well, I finish here at six," proffered Stuart.

"I'll meet you outside Costa at six-thirty if that is alright."

"By the way, I'm Stuart, what is your name?"

"Angela," the girl answered.

"Well, Angela, I'll look forward to it." Stuart smiled. He was on the up and up again.

At six-thirty Stuart met Angela. She had put on a pretty blue dress and redone her hair. They had coffee and Stuart asked if she would like to return to his studio flat. Angela readily agreed and said tentatively, "I'm very good at massage."

Stuart thought this sounded hopeful and said, "Well I'll take off my shirt when we get in and we'll see."

Stuart drove her in his van to the flat. "I have a van for convenience," he explained.

"Your flat is rather small," complained Angela, when they arrived.

"I don't want to be bothered with domestic chores," replied Stuart. "Look, I'll lie on the bed on my stomach. I have some body lotion and we'll see what you can do."

Angela was a little taken aback at the immediate presumption of this. No offer of a drink, and she had to take her own coat off.

Stuart found the body lotion and lay on his bed on his stomach. Angela was not happy about all of this and wished she hadn't mentioned a massage. She wanted some conversation, and then perhaps some kissing and petting. This all seemed so clinical.

Stuart just lay there obviously waiting for the massage. Angela shrugged to herself and took the body lotion from Stuart.

He had stripped down to his underpants, but Angela still had her dress on, having draped her coat on a chair.

She started to massage his shoulders, but her reluctance must have showed.

"You are digging in your nails," complained Stuart.

Angela tried again to massage his neck but she did not have her heart in it.

"You are hurting me," Stuart seemed to snarl. Then he shouted, "Do you really know what you are doing, you stupid girl?"

That did it. Angela threw the body lotion on the floor, snatched up her coat and left.

"No one is going to talk to me like that," she thought. "Selfish creature." She let herself out and decided to go back to her own place, walking.

Stuart sat up. "Well that's that," he thought. "That didn't last long!"

He decided to get dressed and went to another pub for a drink and a smoke. An old acquaintance of his was there and went up to him.

"Interested in buying some cannabis?" he enquired.

"How much?" asked Stuart.

"£100 and that's cheap. You could sell it on for more."

Stuart had five twenty-pound notes in his wallet. He took them out and handed them over. The cannabis was in a packet. Nothing more was paid.

Stuart moved onto the next pub, 'The Dog and Whistle', and fortunately there were some old mates he had known from the past. He soon sold all the cannabis and made £100 profit.

Stuart chortled to himself. "That was easy," he thought. "Better than the railway and easier money than stacking shelves."

The next day he gave in his notice at the supermarket. It was with immediate effect. He made up some story that he had an aching shoulder and could no longer do the work.

He went back to the pub where he had purchased the cannabis. The same guy was there. "I could purchase £200 worth if you have it," he declared. The guy had a large black shoulder bag.

"Come outside," he said.

Outside, round a corner, he produced a larger packet. Stuart handed over the £200. He returned to The Dog and Whistle. Word must have got around, because very soon the whole amount had been sold for £400.

This pattern continued for several weeks, and soon Stuart had quite a large amount of money. There seemed to be no lack of willing customers, but they all understood the need for secrecy.

CHAPTER 14

Some of his customers were so needy they referred to him as 'Sir' and others began to invite him to their drinks parties. He seemed to be becoming some form of celebrity and he loved it. At last he felt in charge and he felt a true person. He did think, however, that he should have some form of employment as a cover, but he was enjoying himself too much to think too seriously about this.

Chapter 15

One evening Stuart was invited to the home of a wealthy client. He was holding a barbecue and drinks party in the home on the Isle of Wight. The party spilled over onto a terrace and the large garden. Some weed was being smoked, but in the grounds and not openly.

There was a group of ladies on the terrace and they were drinking gin and tonics. Stuart's wealthy client came over to him.

"These ladies have organised parties in the past for me but not this one. I have organised this myself, but I value them and have invited them to enjoy an evening away from work. Let me introduce them."

"Stuart, this is Leanne, this is Rosa, this is Amelia and this is Annabelle."

"Ladies, this is Stuart, a good friend of mine."

The ladies all smiled a greeting, but Stuart was looking into Annabelle's eyes. She was lovely and he felt totally bewitched.

She too looked into his dark eyes and his smile was radiant. The other ladies seemed to notice their mutual attraction and just seemed to drift away.

Stuart wasn't sure how to handle this. Annabelle was lovely, and dressed in a beautiful, obviously designer dress of pale blue silk. Her hair was immaculate and she was wearing an expensive sapphire necklace and bracelet. She wore high heeled shoes which showed off her slim ankles. Fortunately, her glass was nearly empty.

"May I fetch you another glass," enquired Stuart. "A gin and tonic, is it?"

"It is," laughed Annabelle.

When Stuart returned they found two garden chairs upon which to sit.

"Have you known our host long?" enquired Annabelle. "I have organised several parties for him as he said, but I mainly organise the food side."

"Are you a good cook?" Stuart enquired tentatively.

"I am afraid I am," replied Annabelle. "I also organise the food for various clubs, including sailing clubs."

"That sounds wonderful," stuttered Stuart. "But tonight you have a free night."

"I do," replied Annabelle. "My father is looking after my son Justin.

"No husband?" enquired Stuart hopefully.

"Oh no. We split up ages ago. He has given me a large settlement, but the divorce is not yet finalised. I have purchased a nice detached house in Gunnard. We can see the sea from the front terrace."

"That sounds lovely," admitted Stuart. "I only have a small studio flat in Portsmouth, but have come over to the island for this party. Have you eaten?"

"Oh yes. The barbecue was superb. Have you not partaken?"

"I was a little late in arriving," admitted Stuart. "And quite honestly don't really feel hungry."

"Would you like to see my house?" offered Annabelle. "I'm sure that we can slip away."

"Thank you, I would," said Stuart, thinking that he was so fortunate to have this offer.

They both slipped away.

The party was being held at Cowes and it was only a short drive to Annabelle's house. Stuart had driven over on the ferry from Portsmouth to Fishbourne and then to the party. Stuart followed Annabelle in his van. She drove a Mercedes SLK.

When they arrived at the house, Stuart was most impressed. It stood out from the other houses and was surrounded by a lovely garden. Annabelle noticed his expression.

"I do have a gardener," she stated. "Do come inside."

Inside, Stuart was taken aback. The hall was slabbed in marble, white and black tiles. A chandelier hung from the ceiling. She led him into the sitting room, which had an obviously expensive Wilton carpet and antique furniture. He hardly dared to move. Annabelle wasted no time.

"I find you immensely attractive," she murmured, and pulled him close to her.

"And I you," retorted Stuart. "You stood out from the crowd like some beautiful flower. I could not take my eyes off you."

"Nor me you," replied Annabelle.

"Is it love at first sight?" laughed Stuart.

Annabelle was serious. "I think it may be," she said. "After the break-up with my husband I have felt no interest in the opposite sex until now."

"What happened?" asked Stuart. He couldn't imagine anyone not wishing to be with this lovely woman.

"Well, he was a venture capitalist and developed my catering business. I think we just drifted apart."

"But you have a son?"

"Yes, Justin. He attends a private boarding school. He is eleven. He is only home now because he had glandular fever. He is quite well now and will soon be returning to school. My father is keeping him tonight."

"Does your husband see him?"

"Not very often. He is so busy. The good thing is that he is very generous to us and makes me a substantial allowance. It helps me to keep my horse."

"You have a horse!" Stuart expostulated.

"Yes, I keep him in a stable at a nearby farm. I try to see him most evenings and pay a stable hand to look after him."

"Do you ride?"

"Oh yes, I love it. Have you not ridden?"

Stuart felt a bit of an idiot. "No, I'm afraid not."

He realised that he was now in a different world. On impulse Annabelle said, "Why don't you stay with me? I don't know what work you do, but give it up."

Stuart was tempted, but it sounded very high handed.

Annabelle continued. "The farmer needs extra help. You could do that and also look after my horse. We could come to some agreement on salary." She repeated, "Give up your life in Portsmouth and come to me."

Stuart was a little indignant. "I cannot be a kept man as it were."

"Well I have plenty of money from my ex, also I earn good money catering. Don't worry about it. Let's forget all these things at the moment and let's go to bed."

Stuart needed no second invitation. Upstairs was as lovely as downstairs. The bedroom was luxurious with a king sized bed. Annabelle stripped down completely and lay on the bed, smiling. Stuart also stripped and lay beside her. She looked so lovely and he cupped her breasts. She moaned softly and soon he was caressing her body. He touched her thighs and entered her vagina with his fingers. She encouraged him with sighs and moans.

"I am on the pill," she murmured.

Without more ado, forgetting a condom, Stuart entered her and they pulsated together. Annabelle uttered a cry of ecstasy as his penis plunged in and out of her.

"Can I come?" he asked.

Annabelle nodded and Stuart had an orgasm. He kissed her and said, "That was wonderful."

"Me too," Annabelle stated.

They had stayed on top of the bed, but they sank beneath the sheets and cuddled up together. They both slept soundly.

In the morning Stuart said, "I would love to stay here with you. But I would have to give up my studio flat. Also, many of my friends and acquaintances are in Portsmouth."

"Make a new life." Annabelle said drowsily. "I have to get up soon because I have a commitment at the Island sailing club. Shall I see you tonight?"

"Most certainly," said Stuart. "I will return home and sort things out."

Chapter 16

Stuart drove back via the ferry to Portsmouth. He went to his landlord and stated that he could not longer afford the rent, which was a lie of course.

He didn't worry about the deposit. He rounded up some of his mates who helped him to put his possessions in the van and they took it all to a storage unit. He just kept his private possessions such as clothing. He went to the Dog and Whistle and explained to his supplier that he may come in more infrequently, but his friend gave him the name of a supplier in Cowes and the name of the pub he sometimes frequented. Stuart bought £500 worth of cannabis to take with him.

A very busy day, but Stuart caught the seven o'clock ferry back to Fishbourne and was soon knocking at Annabelle's door in Gunnard.

"You've come!" she exclaimed. "Let me introduce you to my son, Justin."

Stuart wasn't too sure about this, but the boy seemed bright and intelligent, and Stuart found him easy to chat to.

"My ex is picking him up tomorrow at seven-thirty and taking him back to school," explained Annabelle.

"I'm sorry that you have been ill," said Stuart.

"Oh, I felt rather rotten, but I'm fine now," replied the boy politely.

Annabelle had a lovely meal prepared of salmon, new potatoes, dill from her garden and peas, and all three ate heartily. For pudding there was strawberries and cream. Stuart was very happy with this excellent meal.

Justin took himself off to his room and Stuart explained what had happened that day. He did not of course tell of the cannabis. Annabelle was very impressed.

"I too have found time to talk to Farmer Giles, he is happy for you to help on the farm, but I shall pay for the time you spend looking after Perseus."

"Perseus?" enquired Stuart.

"My horse, I did mention that."

"Oh yes, of course. Well I know little about farming, but I do learn quickly."

"I will introduce you to Farmer Giles and Perseus tomorrow," offered Annabelle. "Let me pour you a drink whilst I clear away."

Stuart asked for a gin and tonic and Annabelle put the dishes in the dishwasher.

"I do have a help, 'Mrs Tibbs', who comes in the mornings. My ex pays her wages," she volunteered.

"Your ex seems most generous," repeated Stuart.

"Oh, money is no object. He is so very rich. That is why we are not yet divorced. It is all so complicated."

"Would you consider getting back together?" enquired Stuart anxiously.

"Goodness, no. He is a good man and we are reasonably friendly still, but too much water has gone under the bridge. I am sure now that he is definitely seeing someone else."

Stuart felt relieved. He had burned his boats with Portsmouth, rarely saw his mother and stepfather, and only occasionally contacted his sister. This was now a new life.

Chapter 17

The next day, after a night of mutual passionate love, Annabelle introduced Stuart to Farmer Giles and Perseus, before dashing off to her catering commitment.

Stuart wasn't really too sure about farming, but was relieved when Farmer Giles explained that he had a pasteurising plant and bottled his own milk. He sold it to one supermarket and had two milkmen who delivered via a van to customers on the island. Stuart felt that he could help here and maybe even get some extra customers. He also made other dairy products.

Stuart could see that Perseus was well cared for and could see that the stable lad did a good job in feeding the horse, grooming him and cleaning out. There was little here for him to do.

Farmer Giles mentioned a salary that was sufficient for Stuart's needs and explained all that he would have to do. This was all mainly to do with the cows and the ensuing products, which suited Stuart. He didn't think he could cope with any agriculture. Annabelle hadn't mentioned how much she would give him for keeping another eye on the horse, but equally no mention had been made of a contribution towards household expenses. Nothing had been said about shopping or payment towards utilities.

Stuart had the contact from the party for customers for cannabis and in his spare time, as Annabelle was often at work in the evening, he found another supplier and more customers. It was a lucrative pastime, but he kept this side hidden from Annabelle. She just thought he went to the public houses for drinks and male company.

They did talk about finance and they decided that looking after Perseus, as well as the stable lad, could cancel any food purchased. Stuart did make a contribution towards utilities for his own pride, although Annabelle had said it was not necessary but unfortunately he often forgot to do this.

Stuart began to feel that he now really had a good life. He loved living in Annabelle's house. It was certainly an improvement on his studio flat, and the house and area completely different from the council estate on which his mother lived and where he had mainly lived as a child.

Annabelle had many impressive friends, who owned detached houses and many had boats, mainly moored at the East Cowes Marina. Dinner parties were given and Stuart was now in a world of fine china, silver cutlery and cut glasses. His mother had had thick china, mugs and basic cutlery. They had also been hungry on occasions.

It was a new world into which he had entered, and he relished it. At first he was a little shy in such surroundings and was hardly able to enter into the conversation of Annabelle's guests. They were, however, polite and accepted him as Annabelle's partner. His clothing had always been hand-me-downs from his brothers, and then cheap clothing from British Home Stores or from charity shops. Annabelle had quickly changed that and taken him to Fields in Cowes, purchasing him new suits, jackets, trousers and ties.

He even went to work at the dairy (before donning a white overall) in corduroy trousers and a smart jacket.

Mrs Tibbs kept the house immaculate and the gardener did a great job in the garden. The lawn was mowed and bushes trimmed. The problem was Stuart's van, from which he was loathe to part. He did use it to go to the public houses for his business, but if they went out it was always in Annabelle's car. Annabelle decided to buy him a little run about four-seater Ford Escort, but she kept it in her name and paid the road tax and insurance.

Stuart began to feel more important. At first he had been fairly laid back in all dealings with the house, garden and guests. He even barely discussed Justin, but as he grew more confident he began to question and query many matters.

He would ask why certain guests were coming and query what Mrs Tibbs did. He would comment on the food purchased and question items that Annabelle bought for the house or garden.

The one good thing was their love life. Stuart was a passionate lover and Annabelle enjoyed their love making. In bed he was kind and considerate and always made sure that she had an orgasm either before he came or at the same time. Annabelle had a lovely body and perfect breasts for him, and he made love to her frequently.

The main problem was that he had a very short temper. The old prejudices from his childhood had left their mark and he would sometimes become quite irrational. One day, Annabelle put a glass in front of him upon which there was a smudge. He picked it up and shouted, "this glass is filthy, it makes me sick".

Annabelle was stunned. She couldn't believe that all the glasses from which he had drunk in the past had always been perfectly polished. He had told her of his childhood, and she wondered if they even had had glasses at all.

Another time Mrs Tibbs had been ill and unable to come. Stuart, leaving for Farmer Giles, had said to Annabelle, "Sit on the terrace and read a book whilst I am gone." Annabelle had no catering work that day.

"I have to wash up and clean up," she volunteered.

Stuart snapped and swore. "You piss me off sometimes, you are so fussy. Life is for fun." He stormed out.

Annabelle was again stunned. Surely he realised that beds had to be made, dishes put in the dishwasher and things needed to be tidied. There was also dusting to be done.

There was one evening when Annabelle had organised a dinner party for her friends for eight o'clock. Two guests did not appear initially and when they did turn up, Stuart again lost his temper.

"Did you not know the meal was for eight?" he shouted.

The guests apologised and said they had had trouble with their cars.

"Well, you may as well leave," Stuart shouted. "The meal is nearly over."

The guests just smiled at Annabelle and turned away. They left.

After everyone had left, there certainly was an atmosphere. Annabelle turned on Stuart.

"How dare you be so rude to my guests," she cried.

"They were insulting you by being late," Stuart said, "I can't let you be treated like that."

Annabelle was still not pleased, even with this answer.

"You have embarrassed me amongst my friends," she said angrily.

"If that embarrasses you then they are not your friends," replied Stuart angrily and stormed off to bed.

Tensions were beginning to build up in the house.

One day Mr Pullinger, the gardener, brought his dog with him. Normally it stayed at home with his wife but on this particular day she had a hospital appointment.

Stuart had not yet left for work and as he opened the door, the dog (a collie) named Benjie, bounded in.

Stuart was livid. "Get that dog out of here," he shouted. "It could run all over the house. Can't you control your dog?"

Stuart was shouting at the top of his voice. Mr Pullinger came in, put the lead on the dog, turned and left the house.

Annabelle ran after him. "Please stay," she begged.

"I can't be spoken to like that," volunteered Mr Pullinger. "I'm sorry, madam, I will come tomorrow. I had to bring the dog.

Annabelle was mortified. Stuart was beginning to act as if he was master of the house, but Stuart just went to work and made no further mention of the incident. Mr Pullinger did come the next day but told Annabelle that his wife was in hospital for a few days and a neighbour was looking after the dog.

"What is wrong with Mrs Pullinger?" enquired Annabelle anxiously.

"A urinary infection. She is on antibiotics but they are just keeping her in for observation. Nothing to really worry about. I shall visit her this evening. My neighbour is also kindly going to pick her up when she is allowed to return home."

"I do hope all goes well," said Annabelle. "I am so sorry about the previous incident. I love dogs."

Mr Pullinger replied, "I know that, madam. I did bring him just once before and nothing was said. If I may say so, madam, you have a strange companion."

"I know," replied Annabelle. "I can't always understand his moods."

Things began to grate on Annabelle. It was a big house but not a hotel. Stuart seemed to treat it as such.

One day some of the lights went out in the chandelier.
They needed replacing.

"Leave them, I'll do them," volunteered Stuart.

Annabelle did not like to remind him and they did not
get replaced. When Stuart was out she asked the gardener,
Mr Pullinger, to replace the bulbs.

There were several such incidents. Stuart was very
untidy and left clothing on the floor for washing. Mrs Tibbs
took the main laundry to the cleaners who also did washing
and ironing, but not towels, which were often left on the
floor, or underwear.

Annabelle realised that from his home it had probably
been in a bit of a muddle, but she thought that the army
would have taught him some self-discipline and organisation.

He began to criticise items that were left in the fridge and
out of date, and even got cross if she ate a biscuit in bed and
left some crumbs. He smoked cigarettes and often there was
ash not only left in the ashtray but on the floor. He would
also leave cigarette lighters on the floor and sometimes even
in the bed. There seemed to be no logic in his criticisms.

Sometimes if they were watching television she would
start to speak. He would either not reply or say "I am trying
to listen", but he would then speak himself.

Chapter 18

At one dinner party that went well, one of Annabelle's friends stated that they were going on a boating trip to Paris but one of their friends was now unable to help.

"I could help," volunteered Stuart. "I am sure Farmer Giles could manage for a while and the stable boy is fine with Perseus."

"How long is the trip?" enquired Annabelle.

"Oh, a week. We have two important friends with us, a Vice Admiral and a lawyer. My friend Alistair is helping me, but Michael was coming as well."

"I would love to help," answered Stuart.

Annabelle was again nonplussed. It would mean that he would be away for a week and he had not discussed it with her.

"That's fine then," said the guest. "It is rather short notice. We'll see you outside the Royal Yacht Squadron at eight tomorrow."

Stuart was elated. The Royal Yacht Squadron, he thought, and travelling with a Vice Admiral albeit retired. He knew he could soon learn to manage a boat.

After the guests had gone, Annabelle spoke. "What about Farmer Giles?" she enquired.

"Oh you can explain," replied Stuart. "I have always wanted to be involved in boats and this is too marvellous to turn down."

"You'll be away for a week."

"Oh, you can manage. You know you can. You always like to do your own thing anyway."

Annabelle felt snubbed. He was in her house, she did all the cooking, organised the washing, organised the cleaner and gardener. He now had the Ford runabout and he was acting in a high-handed manner.

She felt too tired to argue so they just left the dishes and went to bed, but Annabelle could not sleep. She began to wonder if she had been wise to invite Stuart into her life. She felt that when she had done so, she didn't really know him.

The next morning Stuart was up and out, meeting the owners of the boat Volant.

The owner of the boat, Maximilian (known as Max), was on board, as were the retired Vice Admiral, Harold and the lawyer, Paul. This was their holiday and they were paying Max a considerable amount for the trip. Max mentioned a sum of money to Stuart which made him gasp.

"Well, you can be my bodyguard as well as help me with the boat," volunteered Max. "The boat is equipped with food and drink, but you may need to help to replenish these as well."

"I shall steer the boat (it was a 35 foot motor cruiser) but I shall need sleep. You will take over then."

Max showed Stuart all the controls and it all seemed fairly straightforward. There were life jackets on board and down below adequate sleeping facilities.

"We will need to put into some ports for refuelling of course," added Max.

Stuart just loved the boat Volant. Again, he felt that life was so good to him. The men were well spoken and cultured. Stuart reminded himself that he must not swear. He had a rolled bag with him containing some decent clothes and some old clothes left over from his time on the railway. He had grabbed them when he awoke that morning and had just given Annabelle a hasty kiss before he left. He felt no guilt at leaving her. She had Mrs Tibbs and Mr Pullinger and plenty of friends. She also had her catering commitments which always seemed fairly regular.

"She'll be alright," thought Stuart to himself. "She should be glad that I have this opportunity."

They set off and crossed the Channel. They eventually reached Le Havre where they joined the lower Seine.

Stuart had soon mastered the controls and had done a night at these. There were maps and a computer, but he seemed to have an instinct for navigation. They had stopped at Le Havre for fuel, but then carried on to Rouen. There they stopped, refuelled and went ashore to a large five-star hotel. They washed and dressed suitably, and Stuart here had the best meal of his life with six courses, including oysters and caviar. This was all paid for by Max.

When they reboarded, they came to Paris where once again they dined at a five-star hotel. They moored the boat and Max stated that they were staying at this hotel for a few nights. The hotel was luxurious. Stuart was glad that he had thrown some decent clothes into his bag, and he was able to get some of his other gear laundered. It was the height of luxury for Stuart. To be waited on and treated with such courtesy and politeness. Max, Harold and Paul met some old friends and introduced Stuart, explaining the trip and referred to Stuart as his 'minder'. Stuart did not object to his, although he knew that now he was also often in charge of Volant.

The lifestyle was stunning for Stuart. The hotel was certainly luxurious, and he had a double room to himself that even had a butler.

This was the lifestyle that Stuart had craved. He had hated living on the council estate, but of course had had to make the best of it, even playing and making friends there, but in his heart he had the resentment that had always seemed to flare up. He wondered if his father was living as he was now.

He was careful not to overstep the mark with Max, Harold and Paul, and managed to appear grateful and helpful when he was with them.

They did not see him 'lord' it with the butler, demanding softer towels and a more frequent change of bed linen. He even criticised the ironing of a shirt when it was returned to him on a hanger. He felt that now he deserved only the best.

Too soon the hotel life came to an end and they returned to Volant. Stuart was careful to maintain a subservience to Harold and Paul, knowing in his heart that they had achieved what he could not, nor had not. He wasn't too sure about Max, because he knew that he smoked weed (they had done this together away from the others). Max had his own supply as had Stuart, but he was also careful to be polite as Max was paying his wages.

The trip back was fine from Paris although the Channel was rough on this occasion. It made the trip longer than anticipated.

Chapter 19

When back at Cowes, Stuart was paid handsomely and was sad to say goodbye to Paul and Harold. The good news was that Max said that Stuart had managed the boat well, done more than his fair share of night navigation, and he would call upon him again. Stuart was overjoyed at this.

When Stuart returned to Gunnard, Annabelle was not at all happy.

"You were away for longer than a week," she complained.

"Well, the Channel was rough on the return," stated Stuart.

He threw his bag on the floor. "I am afraid that I have some washing here. The hotel in which we stayed did some, but I still have some clothes now that need washing and cleaning."

Annabelle was furious. "You come in here at nine in the evening. No kisses or affection and just talk about cleaning and washing. You don't ask what I have been doing or how I have been managing."

"There is plenty of time to talk," replied Stuart. "I am sorry, but I am tired. The Channel crossing was difficult. But if you must know we stayed at wonderful hotels and it certainly opened my eyes to what a wonderful life some people live. But come, let's go to bed and make love."

Annabelle relented. She had missed sex with Stuart, and her life had seemed empty without him. She no longer enjoyed sleeping alone.

Stuart was a bright man and realised that Annabelle was not best pleased with his sojourn on the Paris trip.

He put his arm around her and gently led her to the bedroom. He himself undressed her and cupped her breasts in his hands. He laid her on the bed and caressed the mound between her thighs with one hand, whilst divesting himself of his clothes with the other.

He then manipulated her clitoris until he felt the wetness between her thighs. He then entered her and was careful not to climax before her. Afterwards he cuddled her close and murmured words of love. Annabelle drowsily listened as he whispered.

"I love you so much, Annabelle. I had no life before you. You are the most wonderful thing that has ever happened to me."

Annabelle wanted to believe his whispered words. Stuart kept his arm around her and they fell asleep.

The next morning Annabelle arose and made coffee for them both. She quickly sorted out his washing ready for Mrs Tibbs to take most of it to the cleaners. The rest she put in the washing machine. She had no catering commitment that day and thought they could spend a day together.

As she took the coffee into the bedroom, Stuart was looking angry.

"What is it now?" she thought.

"There are biscuit crumbs in the bed."

"They were there last night, but you didn't notice. I ate a few late night biscuits in bed whilst you were away and a few crumbs must have dropped off. The sheets are not dirty but I can get them taken to the laundry today."

"I cannot stand crumbs in the bed," shouted Stuart. "I have noticed it before but managed to say nothing, but it really pisses me off."

Annabelle was shocked. Where was the caring lover of last night? Do you really speak to someone like that if you love them? She put down the coffee for Stuart, but he got up and dressed.

"I suppose I had better see Farmer Giles and your stupid horse," he snarled. "I am tired of dealing in pasteurised milk and certainly fed up with cows. I think that I am going to chuck it all in."

Annabelle felt tearful. "What will you do if you give up your work with Farmer Giles?"

"God knows, but there must be a better life than that."

Stuart went out and slammed the door. Annabelle felt cold with shock. She had put money into his bank for overseeing Perseus, but it was not a great amount. From Farmer Giles's money he had contributed to household expenses occasionally, but sometimes he forgot. Annabelle had noticed a fifty-pound note sticking out of his wallet one day and had wondered from whence it came. She of course knew nothing of his wheeling and dealing in cannabis. He smoked outside the house and she thought that he just smoked ordinary cigarettes.

Mrs Tibbs came and Annabelle apologised for the extra washing. She did change the bed linen and drove Mrs Tibbs in the Mercedes to the laundry herself. Usually, Mrs Tibbs took it in a pull suitcase herself at the end of her shift. Annabelle of course always gave her extra money for this.

Stuart reappeared in time for some lunch (usually Farmer Giles's wife had fed him at midday) and informed Annabelle that he was quitting his dairy work.

"Whatever did Farmer Giles say?" exclaimed Annabelle, horrified at this turn of events.

"I told him to stuff it," retorted Stuart, and refused to say anymore on that subject.

"What about Perseus?"

"Oh, there is the stable lad, but I will continue to keep an eye on him and shall probably be around to get him ready if you wish to go for a ride."

"What do you mean, 'probably be around'?"

"Well I bumped into Max when I went for a coffee after talking to Giles. He says that there is definitely going to be more boat work for me. Several of his acquaintances want trips out in the boat and are willing to pay well. I said I would be happy to help with that. I think boating is more my cup of tea."

Annabelle didn't know what to make of this. Would he be away as before for a week or longer? This wasn't the life she had envisaged with him. He almost seemed now to want a separate life, with sex when he chose.

"Is anything arranged?" she asked tentatively.

"Yes. A couple want to go to Butlers Hard, and stay the night. Max is happy with that.

"When is that?" asked Annabelle.

"Tomorrow actually. I'm going to the pub, The Fox and Hounds, tonight, to meet Max to finalise details."

"What time will you be back tonight?" enquired Annabelle.

"When we've finished talking. Maybe not until the place closes. I will just slip into bed when I come in and try not to wake you."

Annabelle was aghast. Slip into bed. No love making or sex here, she thought. He was taking everything for granted.

"What about our evening meal?"

"Oh, don't worry, I'll have something at The Fox and Hounds. You suit yourself."

This remark 'suit yourself' seemed to be becoming a refrain. It was clear that he was suiting himself. He had made no contribution to the household for some considerable time. He had given her no money from his boat trip, which she knew had proved lucrative, and was still making no offer towards expenses.

Apart from the love making, which now seemed to be more infrequent, and would be more so if he was going on extended boat trips, she felt that things were no better than when she had split with her husband. At least that had been a clean break, and he had been and was still, generous with his money. When they had been together, he had taken her abroad, America, Greece, Thailand, and Singapore, for example, and had given her expensive jewellery. There was the sapphire necklace and bracelet, for example, that she had worn when first meeting Stuart. She still had her engagement ring which was also a huge sapphire surrounded with diamonds. He had given her a lovely ruby and diamond brooch, a gold charm bracelet, to name but some of his presents. Stuart, of course, had given her nothing, not even a small thing, which she would so have appreciated. He had had money from Farmer Giles, plus her small allowance to him of course and could easily have bought her some small gift, such as a silk scarf or even a piece of costume jewellery. It seemed as if he felt that the whole world should revolve around him, and she began to feel very unhappy and depressed.

She had known of course that it would be one sided financially, but she had expected more kindness and consideration from their relationship. Yes, there had been mutual attraction but he too was having sex and orgasms.

She reflected on the situation. He had moved from a seemingly small flat (she had never seen it of course), into the large detached house which she owned outright. He had the comfort of nice surroundings, good meals, bespoke clothes, and no financial worries. She had urged Farmer Giles to employ him, for the sake of his pride and even purchased the Ford Escort for him.

Chapter 20

Annabelle put all events on the scales of justice. What was she getting? Companionship maybe, but that seemed to be thinning out. She had never queried his visits to public houses such as The Fox and Hounds, and of course he always returned to her bed. But she had all the responsibility of running the house, communicating of course with Justin, who seemed to be spending more of his free time from school with his father, and even worse, appearing to be getting more critical of the things that she had to do. He seemed to have no problem in occupying himself in her house if she was on a catering commission. Either going out to the pub or watching the television. She noticed as well that the drinks cabinet was often empty.

Annabelle took a sigh. She thought she would let it ride for a while, and maybe, she thought, hopefully things would get better.

That night Stuart did not come into bed until one in the morning. Annabelle had been unable to sleep. Stuart had obviously had a great deal to drink (he had walked to The Fox and Hounds) and was soon snoring loudly.

The next morning he was up and out to meet Max and his clients. He was obviously at Butlers Hard the next night, and did not return until late evening the next day. Annabelle was home and quickly put together a salad for him.

"How did it go?" she enquired.

"Oh, ok. The woman was a bit of a gas bag and got on my nerves, but her husband was quite interesting to talk to. I think Max wants me permanently to help him with his clients. The money is better than I got from Farmer Giles and with Max I am getting a better lifestyle."

"I thought that was with me," Annabelle managed to say.

"I am grateful for all that you have done for me," Stuart admitted. "You are a wonderful cook, obviously excellent at your catering business, and you have given me a lovely home and introduced me to your friends; but with Max I do feel more independent and he has taken me to some wonderful hotels that I never expected to experience in my wildest dreams. He has opened new doors for me, and quite honestly, as I have said before, the boating world seems to suit me so well."

"Well what about us?" enquired Annabelle.

"I love you," Stuart admitted. "We are good together in bed as well, but I do need some independence. Come, let's go to bed now."

For once Annabelle did not feel in the least bit passionate. Stuart said that he loved her, but he obviously loved himself more, she mused to herself. Of course he was being offered a better and more fulfilling life for himself, but he was still using her house as his base and making use of all the facilities when he was home.

Stuart was frowning. "Don't you want to make love tonight?" he asked.

"Well, if you are going to be away more frequently, it doesn't seem the same as when we were in bed together every night."

"A lot of people live like that," retorted Stuart. "What about sailors on ships, people who go mountaineering, archaeologists, explorers?"

"I didn't think of that when I met you," answered Annabelle. "I had already been with a husband who worked away a great deal and we drifted apart. I don't want that to happen to us."

"It won't," Stuart replied. "I told you, I love you and I'm sure you love me, but I can't live in chains. I love the freedom of being on the sea."

Stuart put his arm around Annabelle and as usual she melted. They went to bed and their love making was as passionate as before.

The next morning Annabelle had a commitment at the Holmwood Hotel in Cowes. They did have their own catering staff, but this was for a big scientific conference and she and her team had been called in to help.

Stuart was still in bed when she got up.

"I've left some muesli and fruit in the kitchen for breakfast," she told him. "I am at work all day and shall not be back until nine. The hotel will do the final clearing up."

"Well, I'm off with Max and some clients to Poole at eleven this morning. We may stay in Poole harbour this evening. I am not quite sure what the arrangements are."

Annabelle's heart sank. Probably another night apart.

"Don't look so glum," said Stuart. "I shall be coming back eventually."

Eventually, thought Annabelle. They were partners but not married. Stuart was acting as if they were an old married couple. She also reflected that he still had made no contribution to the household costs. She had to leave, so could say nothing at this point.

Stuart met Max who this time had three attractive young women with him. One of the ladies explained, "We'd heard of these boat trips and Lisa, my friend, is getting married. This is a little hen party." Max had the boat equipped with food and drink and said that they would indeed be moored in Poole that evening.

The trip was smooth and now Stuart mainly steered the boat. They had refreshments on the way and finally reached Poole. When moored up, all three girls said they wanted to dine at a restaurant. Max and Stuart readily agreed, but one of his friends, Stephanie, seemed to attach herself to Stuart. Max paid for the meal as the fee charged for the trip covered such a cost. There was sleeping accommodation on the boat, comfortable for four but here there were five. Stephanie suggested cuddling up to Stuart, but he stated he would be on deck to guard the boat.

About three in the morning, Stephanie joined him. Without more ado, she hugged and kissed him. Stephanie was a pretty girl and he found himself returning her kisses. But he was careful to take it no further.

"Are you single?" she enquired.

"I have a lady in my life," replied Stuart.

"That's not the same, men often have lots of ladies in their lives. I would like to see you again. Here is my number."

Stephanie wrote her name down, put down her number and drew a big heart underneath. She then returned to the cabin. Stuart was on watch and hardly slept.

The next morning they all returned to Cowes. The girls seemed happy and Lisa paid Max and then paid Stuart.

Stephanie lingered. She jumped and put a kiss on Stuart's face.

"Don't forget what I said," she murmured.

Chapter 21

When Stuart returned that day. Annabelle was home.

He walked in and unpacked his bag that he had had the foresight to take.

"What is that on your face?" Annabelle enquired as she immediately noticed the red lipstick mark.

"Well, it was a small hen party and one of the bride's friends jumped up and kissed me. It didn't mean anything as I wasn't interested."

Annabelle began to feel more concerned and frustrated. Was he going to stray now that he had this new freedom? Justin was coming home to her the next weekend and she must spend time with him. She felt that she couldn't keep worrying about Stuart.

"I am not really happy," she volunteered. "I don't think things are working out as I hoped."

"Don't be silly," retorted Stuart. "Everything is fine."

"No, it isn't," answered Annabelle. And at that moment, unfortunately, Stuart pulled out his handkerchief and the paper with Stephanie's number and the red heart drawn on it fell out.

Annabelle picked it up.

"Is this the girl that kissed you," she enquired.

"Yes, but as I told you it meant nothing."

Annabelle snapped. "You have made little contribution to this house, using it more as a hotel. You have been rude to my friends and now you seem to want your own life. I think it better if you leave."

Stuart looked at her in horror. "We love each other," he exclaimed.

"I thought I loved you," replied Annabelle. "But you are very selfish and thoughtless. I think I want to give more time to my son who is actually coming to me this weekend."

"Are you serious?" said Stuart. "What about our love making?"

"That isn't the end of the world. Kindness and consideration are more important. You are acting as if you own this house and I feel that I am being used. I want you to leave."

"When?" asked Stuart.

"As soon as possible. You can keep whatever I have given you and ironically you have given me nothing. Just take yourself off as soon as possible. Like now."

Stuart was stunned. He had begun to think this Gunnard house was his. He had gotten used to this lifestyle. He probably had sufficient money for a deposit on a flat and he still had some items in store, but he was going back to square one.

Pride took over. He went upstairs, packed some, but not all of his clothes and walked out. He went and found Max.

"I've been kicked out of the house," he stated. "I don't know where I shall sleep tonight."

"You can stay with me tonight," replied Max. "But what happened?"

Stuart didn't really want to go into details.

"One of the hen party girls chased me, but it was nothing. I don't think Annabelle liked me being away on the boating trips."

Max felt a bit responsible here.

"Look, I'm away from my wife, but it's our lifestyle. Lots of men work away from home. Anyway, come home with me tonight and we'll try to sort things out.

Max's wife was sympathetic to Stuart. She didn't know his background and just thought that he had been thrown out in a fit of rage. She gave Stuart a snack and a stiff drink and showed him to a bedroom.

Here Stuart began to think. Should he go back to Annabelle and beg to be taken back? As he thought, however, he realised that the lipstick and note with the heart were just the possible final straw. Yes, he had been away from the home, but as he thought he realised that perhaps he had taken it all for granted. He hadn't been a paying guest, nor a real partner or husband, but as he thought he realised that he had acted as if the house was his and that he could behave however he wished.

Should he go back and offer to make more of a contribution to the household? He decided that he would return in the morning and try. On this thought he went to sleep. The next day he thanked Max and his wife for their hospitality. Max said that he had no commission for a few days, which gave Stuart some space.

He returned to the Gunnard house. Annabelle's son Justin was not in situ, but busy reading.

"Why have you returned?" enquired Annabelle.

"I love you as I have said. If I have made mistakes, I am sorry. Please can we try again?"

"No, definitely not," retorted Annabelle. "When I met you I knew that you had little, and I was more than happy to share what I had, to be with you. Life is not just about sex. You have become domineering and arrogant. You have become to act as if this house is yours and really made little contribution. I don't like your temper and it is better for us to part before things get even worse."

Stuart began to feel angry. "You invited me into your home."

"Yes, I did, but you have taken advantage of that fact. I don't want to spend my life worrying when you are coming in or what mood you will be in. Several of my friends have complained about your rudeness. The time has come for us to part. I think, Stuart, that you are your own worst enemy. Goodbye."

Stuart was now too angry to argue further. He was what he was and that was it. He turned and left.

CHAPTER 21

He drove his van onto the next available ferry and returned to Portsmouth. He went to see his mother and stepfather.

Chapter 22

He had almost forgotten what his mother's house looked like or the area. He hated it as he drove up. His mother was delighted to see him, but there were now half-brothers and a sister that he barely knew. His stepfather was king but NOT HIS father. He heard that Catherine had moved so far away, contact had been lost.

He slept on the settee that night and the next day drove to Portsmouth University. He had come to this decision suddenly overnight. He felt that his life needed another direction after the shock of being asked to leave Gunnard. The bursar was kind and put him in touch with the appropriate hierarchy. He spent the day producing documents from his army career, and it was decided that he could commence studying at the beginning of the university year which was only in two weeks' time. He had decided to study creative writing as he enjoyed words and their many uses. He returned home but was soon back at the campus seeking accommodation. Fortunately, there was a study available. It was small but had a single bed, cupboards and a desk. It even had an ensuite shower.

This was fine, but he had to go to several council offices and talk to several councillors to obtain a grant. He was good now at talking and persuasion, and managed to obtain a sum of money that had somehow been unclaimed. It had been donated to the university for a deserving cause for education by a charitable donor, but had been left in abeyance.

He stayed with his mother and stepfather for a week, but was allowed to take up his study a week before the term commenced. He was elated with his success at obtaining university entrance plus a grant at such short notice, but still felt very bitter and bewildered at his banishment from Gunnard. He tried to focus on the tasks ahead and tried not to dwell too much on his loss.

Amazingly, in the study adjacent to his, a young pretty lady emerged from the room. Skilled at making contact, Stuart introduced himself. The young lady smiled at him and stated that her name was Francesca. She stated that she had made a late decision to attend the university, but it was obvious that she was only in her early twenties. She said that she had been bringing things from her home which was in Portsmouth to her room at the college and was looking forward to the new term. She added that she was reading Education as she hoped to become a teacher.

Stuart acted quickly and asked her if she would care to go for a drink with him. Francesca agreed and soon they were in another pub, not frequented by him previously, The White Swan.

Stuart did not smoke and decided to only do a little wheeling and dealing if absolutely necessary and to smoke as little now as possible. Unfortunately, one of Stuart's old customers was in The White Swan. They made eye contact, but Stuart glared at him and the guy moved away when he noticed that Stuart was accompanied by a female.

The evening went well but Stuart decided to play the gentleman. He drove Francesca back to her parents' house, saying that he looked forward to seeing her at the university the following week. Francesca was of slight build with dark curly hair similar to his. He felt an immediate attraction but decided to see how it panned out.

His mother was delighted that he had obtained a place at university and amazed how quickly he had managed to get it all organised.

Stuart thought he would try once more, however, at Gunnard and see if the fact that he was going to attend university would improve his chances of salvaging the situation. Perhaps this had been in his mind all along after he was asked to leave. He thought that maybe it elevated him in society and maybe would elevate him in Annabelle's eyes.

He drove over one evening before the term started, hoping that she would be in. He knocked at the door and Annabelle answered.

"May I come in?" he enquired.

"Why have you come? I don't want you here."

"May we talk?"

Annabelle relented and stepped back from the door so that he could come in. Justin was not there.

"Well?" she asked.

"I have obtained a place at Portsmouth University. I thought that may interest you."

"I am pleased for you, Stuart, but it is not my concern. I just wish you every success."

"I could come back here at weekends or at least occasionally."

"No, Stuart, you will not change. I am sorry but as I have said before in different words, you are selfish and egotistical. You will always have an eye for the ladies, and I don't want all the uncertainty of your behaviour in my life."

Stuart could see that Annabelle was adamant. He looked around the room. He had so much enjoyed living in the house. It still looked elegant and tasteful. He looked at Annabelle. She was an attractive woman and he remembered with regret their passionate love making. He realised, however, that there was now no going back.

"Thank you for all that you did," he said sadly. "I realise that I blew it and I'm so sorry that I caused you any anguish." He made to give her a farewell kiss, but she drew back.

"Goodbye Stuart," she said. "Good luck." So saying, she stepped away for him to leave.

Stuart drove away, this time sadly. He realised that he couldn't turn the clock back and wondered if he could really change himself. He decided not to return to his home but to take up residence in his study at the university.

Chapter 23

When the term started Stuart enjoyed some of the lectures but felt that in some ways his knowledge was superior to theirs. He was quickly elected as student spokesman, maybe because he was older and certainly loquacious.

He enjoyed the extensive library at the university and found it easy to write his essays. His brain had always had the capacity to easily absorb knowledge and he enjoyed letting his brain roam over all types of writing and literature.

He saw Francesca around the university and met her occasionally as she was going into her room. He managed to sit next to her sometimes in the refectory and bumped into her in the kitchen that was on their landing. He still held back from making an obvious advance, although he realised that he was missing a sex life. All work and no play was not really for him.

The beds in the study were only three foot wide and he couldn't imagine passionate sex for a whole night in such constraint. However, being Stuart, one day as Francesca was about to enter her room with several books underneath her arm, Stuart smiled and took the books from her.

"Let me carry those in for you," he offered.

As they entered Francesca's room, Stuart put down the books and drew her to him. He stroked her face and kissed her. Francesca did not draw away, but kissed him in return.

They were soon on Francesca's bed, and soon Stuart was caressing her breasts, after undoing her bra. She clung to him and quickly Stuart undressed. He had been without sex for so long he quickly put his hand between her thighs.

"Are you on the pill?" he enquired hastily.

"Yes, yes," she gasped as without hesitation he entered her. They climaxed together quickly and Stuart immediately felt guilty at the speed with which it had all taken place. He liked the girl, but really hardly knew her or anything about her. It certainly wasn't the intensity of feeling that he had always had for Annabelle.

Francesca redressed and sat down on the bed.

"Gosh!" she said, "That was so quick. I didn't think we were going to go all the way."

Stuart wondered if this was a reprimand. "I'm sorry," he retorted. "But I just got carried away. You are a lovely girl."

Francesca smiled. Stuart knew of course that she was no virgin, and she had certainly been as keen as he.

"I must get on with my essay," Francesca said.

"Oh yes, me too. But I do hope we can meet up again."

"I'm sure we will," Francesca agreed.

Back in his study, Stuart was thoughtful. He knew that he would probably never again feel the same affection with a girl that he had felt with Annabelle.

"Why was I such an idiot?" he moaned out loud. "Why, oh why. I had it all and threw it away."

All his old bitternesses from life reared up in his head and he left his study and went back to The Fox and Hounds. He purchased some more cannabis and smoked several joints. He then moved on to yet another public house, 'The Taverner's Rest', where he had sold some of the cannabis that he had purchased. He always carried some cash with him these days but now he had more. He felt a little guilt knowing that he had virtually been sponsored through the university out of charity, but he managed to dispel these thoughts. "Life is for living," he said to himself, "and hang the world."

Feeling better within himself he returned back to his study and managed to toss off two essays. One on the mental therapy of creative writing and one on its early development.

Chapter 24

S tuart continued with his studies but saw little of Francesca. He didn't feel ready for a long relationship, and she appeared to be finding other boyfriends. He saw different male students enter her room and he didn't think that that was for academic discussion.

Stuart was able to complete his degree within eighteen months. He did hire a cap and gown to receive his degree but then puzzled as to his next move. Returning to his study he saw Francesca. She was crying by her door.

"Whatever is wrong?" he asked. "What has so upset you?"

"I hardly dare tell you."

"Tell me. I can keep a secret."

"It won't be a secret for long. I am pregnant."

Stuart looked at her in amazement. "When we had sex, you told me that you were on the pill."

"I was, but I ran out of them and with all the work at university I forgot to get a repeat prescription. When I did remember it was too late. I thought that I was just run down from overwork when I didn't have my periods."

"What are you going to do?" enquired Stuart.

"Well, they have let me accelerate my course to complete my degree and I have finished the examinations."

"I didn't see you at the ceremony."

"No, I didn't go. I shall get my degree in the post. I am going to get my teaching certificate after the baby is born."

"You are going to have it?"

"Oh yes. I honestly don't know who the father is, so there's no help there, but my parents are supportive. My father is quite wealthy, he deals in antiques and he has purchased a bungalow for me."

"Gosh!" exclaimed Stuart. "Is it in Portsmouth?"

"Yes, I hadn't even seen it when he bought it and Mother has already got it furnished."

"Didn't they want you to have the baby whilst living with them?"

"No, they are a bit old fashioned and after they got over the shock they thought I should have some independence. If I continue with my plan to do a postgraduate certificate of Education, my mother will help with looking after the baby."

"What about finance?"

"Well, I shall get a grant and my parents are giving me an allowance. It will cover the outgoings from the upkeep of the bungalow."

Stuart made a hasty decision. "I could come and live with you," he offered. "But why were you crying?"

"Well, I told one of the possible fathers and he was quite rude. He said that he was only one of many and to some extent that is true."

"When is the baby due?" asked Stuart. He noticed now that she did indeed wear a loose flowing dress and that there was indeed a baby bump.

"I don't show much," stated Francesca. "But I am actually seven months pregnant."

"Good Lord," exclaimed Stuart. "I am sorry but I hadn't noticed. We haven't exactly seen much of each other in the last months. You probably went home but I preferred to stay here and do some private studying. What are you going to do now?"

"Well, I shall go to the bungalow."

"Let me drive you. I can also put some of our gear into my van. I didn't actually know where or what I was going to do next, but hey ho. I shall be happy to accompany you and we can see where we go from there."

Francesca agreed. She was in a complete turmoil and was glad to have his company.

Chapter 25

Stuart drove Francesca to the bungalow, which was in a leafy part of Portsmouth in a nice road lined with trees. It was small but had a pleasant outlook onto a meadow at the rear, and a small compact garden.

Inside it was modern with a compact kitchen, two living rooms and two bedrooms, one ensuite, and a decent sized bathroom with toilet and shower. Stuart felt really at home. It wasn't as grand as Gunnard, but certainly better than his mother's home and in a much more salubrious area.

"I would like to stay," he offered. "I can contribute to the maintenance."

"Oh! What will you do for work? Have you been offered employment?"

Stuart became vague. He could hardly admit to drug dealing, but said, "Well I was in the army and then employed working as the skipper of a boat."

"Oh, that sounds exciting, can you take that up again?"

"I don't think so. The regulations for skippers are now very detailed and I fear that I would no longer be able to do the work. There are so many boxes that have to be ticked, such as first aid knowledge and navigation qualifications needed that I do not have, but do not worry I shall get by."

Francesca accepted this. Her parents were supportive but their disappointment in her, however, was obvious, despite the fact that they would have a grandchild.

They had wanted her to stay on at university for the postgraduate certificate of Education and maybe meet some nice young man and marry as was the case in their day. But times change and they had supported their daughter in every way that they could.

Francesca could still feel in their manner towards her, however, a slight resentment, and felt that Stuart could offer a buffer against this.

"How could you cope with a baby and the house?" enquired Francesca.

"Oh, I'm adaptable. I shall probably be out quite a bit, and maybe find some alternative employment. Look, I'll go shopping and let's start from there."

They put their belongings down and Francesca showed Stuart to one of the bedrooms. It was obviously not the one in which she was going to sleep.

Stuart accepted this. After all, he had nothing to lose and nowhere else to go.

"I have fallen on my feet again," he mused to himself.

Chapter 26

S tuart settled well into the bungalow, but there was no love making. Stuart didn't fancy making love to a pregnant girl and they stayed in their separate bedrooms. He often went out in the evening, wheeling and dealing in cannabis, but did undertake shopping for food and mowed the lawns at the house. Francesca's parents tended to avoid him and this suited him fine. She visited her parents but once they knew that he was in residence they ceased calling.

Francesca and Stuart were living amicably together and when Francesca's waters broke Stuart drove her to the hospital. Fortunately, it was a short labour and she gave birth to a baby girl. Stuart visited every afternoon and Francesca's parents visited in the evening.

Stuart smiled wryly as he was certain that the nurses in the maternity unit thought the baby was his.

When it was time for Francesca to return home, her mother brought the cot and pram round to the house. She had already purchased these but kept them at the family home. She also brought baby clothes and Pampers. Francesca hadn't prepared a nursery, so these were all placed in her bedroom.

Stuart began to feel irritated with the crying of the baby and the regular feeding necessary. Francesca said that she was going to call the child Sylvia, but there were no plans for a christening.

Stuart began to stay out of the house more frequently. He came in late at night but the baby always seemed to be crying.

He decided to take on some work offered by an acquaintance which involved renovating an old farmhouse. He was given carte blanche for this, and enjoyed being his own person away from the baby, who seemed to occupy Francesca night and day.

The work was well paid as the owner of the property paid regularly and was very definite in his requirements. The owner was a retired dental surgeon, now a widower, but who wished to enjoy his retirement in this renovated property. The work lasted for nearly a year and then, happy with the work, Stuart had a further recommendation from the dentist's friend. This time it was the conversion of an old farm barn on the outskirts of Portsmouth. Stuart enjoyed driving into the rural atmosphere and away from Francesca and the child. He began to think that perhaps he should find a place of his own as he still had items from his studio flat in storage. He had kept up the rent on this and the few possessions he had had were still in safe storage. It was easy, however, to go back to the bungalow and Francesca was a good cook. He nearly always had a good breakfast and evening meal before he went out again in the evening.

Time went by and soon the child was crawling and then walking.

Stuart had grown fond of Francesca but she was totally absorbed with the child. She suddenly announced that Sylvia needed a bed and really they needed Stuart's room. Stuart once again felt rejected, but he too had begun to feel more and more that this household was no longer for him. He knew that Francesca had plans to take up her option on the postgraduate certificate at the university now and that her mother was willing to babysit rather than Francesca having to pay a crèche or nursery fee.

Stuart decided to take a reconnoitre of his situation. Firstly, he went to the storage unit where some years back he had stored his belongings to move in with Annabelle. He had a shock, however. The owner of the unit said that all within had gone for auction due to lack of payment. Stuart realised that he must have forgotten to maintain the payments due to his admission to university and the difficulties in obtaining a grant. He realised that he had sometimes forgotten to read his post or even to notify the relevant people of his various changes of address. He had been lax and now it was too late.

He began to examine his finances. Yes, he had been paid well for his last two jobs and completed, but he had spent liberally on drink and cannabis and with the cannabis he realised that he was owed money from prior transactions, which again he had let slip. He had given money to Francesca for his keep and purchased groceries, but he realised that he had been 'Jack the lad' in the pubs, often buying drinks for others. He certainly did not have the money that he now needed to make a fresh start.

He began to inquire into the cost of renting a flat but after visiting several estate agents in Portsmouth, he realised that rents had drastically increased. Larger deposits were needed and the rules for renting had changed. A large sum had to now be handed over through an agent and held in case of damage or misuse of a flat.

He realised that he would certainly have to cash in his small army pension and clear out his small bank account.

He promised Francesca that he would find somewhere else to live, but there was a strong degree of uncertainty in his mind. He decided to drive over to the Isle of Wight where possibly accommodation would be cheaper.

One estate agent in Cowes had a basement flat that was in his financial range. He hastily agreed to this, sight unseen.

He returned to Portsmouth and released all his cash, cashing in his pension and going slightly into the red at the bank.

He informed Francesca that he would leave at the end of the week but hoped that they would always remain friends. He had actually grown fond of Sylvia. She was a quaint little thing and could be very endearing, but he knew that he could not have made any permanent commitment as he would always be number two in the relationship and that would certainly not suit him. He also felt, that although fond of the child, he was not father material. The shock of his own father's desertion had never really left him, and he had the fear that some of his father's failings could be in his genetic make-up.

He returned to the Isle of Wight and managed to stay in a small hotel until he obtained the keys to his basement flat. He visited the council offices in Newport and after due diligence in examining his finances, he was informed that he could, through benefits, have a reduction in the rent.

When he visited the flat it was indeed a basement. The view was a brick wall only metres from the kitchen window. The previous renter had left carpet down, but it was badly stained. The kitchen floor and bathroom floor were covered in stained linoleum. The bathroom suite itself was in a hideous avocado green which he hated on sight. The kitchen was small, but there was no oven, although the previous renter had left the microwave, possibly because second-hand electrical goods were not saleable. The living room did have a reasonably large window, but again with no view. Stuart shuddered. It was all so depressing.

Using the cash he carried with him, he went into Cowes and purchased a very cheap basic bed which was to be delivered within two days. He visited the charity shops and from one run by the RSPCA, managed to find a new duvet and some new pillows. He went to the Earl Mountbatten shop and purchased some items of furniture, china, glass and cutlery. These he managed to put into his van.

He arranged the furniture and sorted out the kitchen utensils, but the bed of course had not yet been delivered. For the first night he slept on the floor but fortunately the bed was delivered the very next day.

When it was installed, Stuart looked round. It seemed as if he was back in the Bronx, back to the beginning.

He knew that he could earn money via cannabis, but that was rather hit and miss. Some of his previous customers had relied on credit and he had been let down. This couldn't happen again. He felt that he had lost the will to obtain further employment.

He sighed as he looked around his flat. It somehow still looked grubby and depressing. Stuart also realised that the one thing he was missing was female company and a sex life. Nothing had reoccurred with Francesca after their initial encounter but at least it had been female company. He realised that he should do something about this.

Chapter 27

Stuart was not happy in his flat and wondered how he could in fact invite a female home. He soon built up a group of men willing to pay for cannabis and was headhunted as it were by a supplier. In England it was still against the law to traffic in the drug, but the dealing was all done very much undercover. Soon some of the men would come to his basement flat and they would either purchase the drug or just sit and smoke. Stuart usually offered drinks as well but included the cost in the charge for cannabis.

One day one of his clients informed him that a friend had died, leaving a rich wealthy widow.

"How does that concern me?" enquired Stuart.

"Well, I could introduce you. She is attractive and you say that you miss female company."

A blind date was set up and the widow, in her fifties, was attracted to the dark handsome looks of Stuart. He wasn't quite so sure as he had had so many rejections. He certainly couldn't invite her round to his flat, but he had money in his pocket and asked her out for a meal at The Duke of York in

Cowes. The lady, Veronica, agreed, and a pleasant evening was passed. Stuart was careful in his conversations, but did say that he had a university degree.

Veronica invited him round to a meal in her house. It was a lovely house in Baring Road, not far from a park, Northwood Park in Cowes. It was pleasantly furnished, and the meal was superb. Stuart was at his most charming. Veronica stated that she had a daughter, but she had married an Australian and was now living in Sydney. She felt that the journey was too far to travel. Veronica talked of her husband, a retired bank manager, who had sadly died from pancreatic cancer. Stuart kept up the charm, but was slightly bored with the conversation.

He certainly couldn't talk at length about his previous lady friends.

He just managed to listen and smile agreeably but was brought down to earth with a jolt when Veronica asked where he lived.

"Oh, along Queens Road in a flat," he said. "It's lovely being so close to the sea. The Royal Yacht Squadron is only a short step away."

"How lovely," stated Veronica, but then added, "I am lonely in this big house. I really miss my daughter and now of course my husband. Would you consider moving in here?"

Stuart was dumfounded. "We hardly know each other," he stuttered.

"Well, you could be a sort of lodger until we see how it works out. Let me show you round the house."

Stuart was almost reeling with shock. Veronica showed him around the house. It was perfect. Four bedrooms, two ensuite, a lovely drawing room next to the dining room and a very modern kitchen. The garden was well tended with lawn and flower beds.

"It is lovely," said Stuart. "I'm not sure, however, that I wish to give up my flat."

"Well don't. Come when you wish. I shall be so glad of the company."

Stuart was unsure how this arrangement could work. Yes, it was a lovely house and he really hated his basement flat, but he now had a whole group of fellow smokers who paid over the top for cannabis just to have a refuge in which to drink and smoke.

He decided to hedge his bets. "Well, I will try to come as often as I can," he conceded. "You are a very charming lady and I do enjoy your company." Here Stuart lied, because he had felt the conversation stilted and because of his reticence rather one sided.

"Are you sure?" he puzzled. "You know very little about me."

"Oh I can make instant decisions," answered Veronica. "You are clearly clever, you have a degree and my friends say that you are unmarried and live alone. It makes sense for lonely people to be together."

Stuart wasn't too sure about this. "Where would I sleep if I stayed?" he stated, wondering what was really in her mind.

"Well there are three spare bedrooms, one of which you could use if you chose to spend a night here."

Stuart breathed a sigh of relief. He didn't wish to rush into a sexual encounter with this woman. He wasn't even sure if he fancied her. She was pleasing to look at. Her dark hair was taken back from her face, showing off her high cheekbones. She dressed well and had a good figure, but he really liked his women now younger with maybe a ponytail and having more exuberance. He didn't think that this would be like his life with Annabelle.

However, he thought wryly, beggars can't be choosers, so he agreed to see Veronica once in a while, but would probably not stay for a night.

Chapter 28

S tuart bought himself a new blazer from a shop in
Newport, and also purchased new trousers, a shirt
and tie from another shop. He decided to invite
Veronica out for a meal and see if he really could live with
her. It seemed rather clinical, but life had made him selfish.

Veronica readily agreed when he called round the same
week, dressed in his new clothes. When he had met Veronica
for the first time, he had worn jeans and a silk patterned
shirt, but that had not seemed to bother her. Now, when he
appeared looking so smart, she smiled.

"It's lovely to see you," she said. "Do come in and have
a coffee."

Over coffee Stuart served his invitation for the following
evening. He began to warm to the lady. The conversation
was not personal and centred mainly on events that
occurred in Cowes.

When Stuart left, he felt that maybe he could move in. It
was certainly better to be living there than his basement flat.

The meal the following evening also went well. It was excellent food at a nearby hotel which Stuart had booked earlier. Veronica looked lovely. She wore a pink lace dress and wore high heeled nude coloured court shoes. She smiled and was engaging in her conversation, chattering about a cruise she had been on and her association with a literary society in Cowes. Stuart was able to talk of his life at Portsmouth University and the content of some of his lectures. He did not, of course, mention Francesca.

When it became time to leave Veronica invited Stuart back to her house for a drink.

Stuart drove her home in his vehicle and willingly agreed. He really began to like this lady and she looked so lovely in her pink dress.

After a gin and tonic, Stuart felt very relaxed in her drawing room. Veronica sat with him on the settee. He had already had wine with the meal and the gin and tonic had been a large one. He wasn't sure now about driving back to his flat.

Veronica refilled his glass. The world became very rosy and Stuart put his arm around her. Veronica rapidly responded and put her head on his chest. Stuart had been without sex for quite a while and all his instincts took over. He began to massage her breasts and she moaned with pleasure.

"Stay the night," she urged.

Stuart needed no further encouragement. They went upstairs together and straight into what was obviously her bedroom.

Veronica slipped out of her dress and actually undressed Stuart, who was only too happy for this to happen. Once in the bed, Veronica caressed his body and he hers. She was indeed shapely and Stuart soon entered her and rapidly climaxed. Veronica, he knew had not done so, and he apologised for his lack of control. Veronica did not seem at all concerned about this but seemed happy when they just cuddled up together.

Stuart made a snap decision the next day. "I would like to move in with you," he said. "But I would still like to keep my flat on for some independence."

"That is fine," smiled Veronica. "My husband left me well provide for financially, so you need make no contribution."

"That does not seem right," argued Stuart. "I must contribute at least to food."

"Very well, if that makes you happy."

They made love again in the large six foot bed. Stuart began to feel that all was getting right in his world. He realised that he would have to stop dealing in cannabis and in any case, some of his customers had become very unreliant with cash. Their promises of payment had not come to fruition and Stuart could not harass them in case the situation became public. He resolved to leave it all behind and just smoke cigarettes.

"I'm afraid I smoke," he confessed.

"Well, that is alright, my late husband smoked a pipe. It is bad for your health, as you know."

"I will try to cut down," he resolved. "I must get back to my flat now. But I will be round this evening."

Stuart returned to his flat and made some hasty phone calls. Some clients were very hostile in their responses and some just cut off his phone call in disgust.

He visited the public house in the evening and when approached made it clear that all drugs and drug dealing had ended. Again, he sensed hostility and was glad to drive round to Veronica.

He had given her no time for his arrival but she soon produced sandwiches and coffee.

"My husband drove a Mazda," she stated. "It is still in the garage. I haven't had the heart to sell it and very rarely drive myself now. Would you like to drive it?"

Stuart was again reluctant. He liked his old van but realised that Veronica would probably prefer to be driven in a car.

Veronica led him round to the double garage at the side of the house. It was a two-seater Mazda and was in a brilliant shade of red. "I will put you as a named driver on the insurance," she offered. "Would you like to drive it now?" Veronica had the keys in her hand. "Why don't we go for a drive?" she suggested.

Stuart got into the car and backed it out of the garage.

Veronica got in. They put on the seat belts and Stuart drove into Newport, the capital of the Isle of Wight. It was an easy car to drive and there was a good working radio.

"It's a very nice car," Stuart said, "but what about my van? I am very fond of it and don't wish to sell it. Anyway, it may come in useful."

"Put it in the double garage," offered Veronica. "And then you will not need to worry about leaving it outside. I take it your flat does not have garage space."

"No, I'm afraid not," said Stuart. "I'm afraid my flat is in a basement and very confined," he at last admitted.

"Well, I will put you as an additional driver on my insurance tomorrow. Use the Mazda and leave yours in the garage."

Stuart was tempted and agreed. Things were happening very fast but he really did like the car.

Stuart drove Veronica home and then drove his van back to his flat. He began to feel the need to smoke some weed and actually began to feel unwell. Stuart knew there were drugs to stop smoking but decided to be strong willed and just gradually cut down.

He lit a rolled cigarette of tobacco and cannabis but made up his mind to smoke only one at this time. He began to think seriously about his life. He realised that he had been very selfish and still regretted the breaking up with Annabelle. He admitted to himself that he had on occasions been arrogant and overbearing. He had taken too much for granted and he didn't want this to happen again with Veronica. She was obviously a good woman and he certainly didn't wish to ruin her life.

"Should I walk away?" he asked himself. But then he thought of the alterative – continuing with cannabis and just having sex with various women – a playboy in fact. "No," he thought. "I do not wish to spend the rest of my life like that."

Thus resolved, he drove back to Veronica, parking his van on the drive. He knocked at the door, but to her horror found her in tears.

"What is wrong?" he asked as he walked in.

To his amazement one of his old customers was in the sitting room.

"I have come to warn Veronica about you," the man said angrily. "I have told her of your drug habit."

"Well, you are a fine one to talk," said Stuart. "You still owe me money."

"I owe you nothing. I threw the last lot down the drain. I was coughing so much and getting chest pains. My wife has helped me and now I'm clean from the stuff. My wife knows Veronica from the literary society and has sent me to warn her away from you."

Stuart felt one of his red rages coming over him. He wanted to knock the fellow to the ground but somehow, he didn't quite know how. He turned away from the room to leave.

Veronica came after him. "Don't go," she pleaded. "I really feel that we can have a life together."

"He's only after your house," his old acquaintance called out. "See sense, he is a playboy, certainly not husband material."

"Husband," thought Stuart. "Husband, such a thought had not entered his head.

He again made a sudden decision. Why not? It was time he acted responsibly and Veronica certainly didn't deserve this oaf ranting at her, wife at the literary society or not.

"I think you should ask him to leave," Stuart said quietly.

"I'm going," called the man as he pushed past them. "Don't say we haven't warned you," he added to Veronica and left.

Stuart took Veronica's hand. "I have smoked cannabis," he admitted, "but I have resolved to cut down and quit. I made that decision before I even came here today. You are a good woman, and deserve a good man. I know that I am not perfect but I will try to improve. I can't live with you without contribution. Just buying food is insufficient. I will find odd jobs and take them, giving you the money from them willingly. The word husband has been mentioned. You deserve stability. Veronica, will you marry me?"

Veronica looked at him. She had probably fallen for him on sight and although she had had no orgasms, enjoyed his closeness and his love making. She was old fashioned at heart and didn't wish just to be an occasional partner.

Without hesitation she said 'yes'. Stuart took her hand and led her back to her bedroom. He just kissed her and they cuddled up together.

"It will take a while," he murmured into her ear. "But I will register it tomorrow in Newport. Are you happy just to have a registry office wedding?"

"I am," said Veronica. "My parents paid for a very big wedding when I married Horace. We had a church wedding and over two hundred guests at the reception at the Holmwood Hotel. But now I would like to keep it simple. I know that there have to be witnesses, but two of my friends from the literary society will help us, I know."

They both fell asleep, but Stuart slept with his arm around Veronica.

Chapter 29

S tuart kept up his promise to himself to reduce the smoking. He even found a few temporary jobs trimming bushes in private gardens, repairing fences and then laying a patio.

Stuart took Veronica into Newport in the Mazda and he bought a wedding ring only.

The day came for their wedding. Veronica looked lovely in a white two-piece suit with a matching hat. Stuart still wore his blazer but sported new trousers and a tie. The ceremony was brief, but with the two witnesses who had agreed to be present, they all had a meal later at the Smoking Lobster in Cowes. Stuart drove them in his van to and from the ceremony. It was his van, his wedding, his day, as well of course Veronica's, but she understood his pride.

There was no honeymoon, but they returned to the house where Veronica had prepared a cold collation. The ladies acting as witnesses were still with them and Stuart had purchased champagne for the celebration. The ladies left in their own cars parked on the large drive, but Stuart had previously thanked them so much for their kindness and given them each a bottle of champagne to take home.

From waving them off Stuart came and knelt on one knee before Veronica. He had grown to love this good kind woman. He hadn't always been able to give her sexual satisfaction, but he had managed many times to control his passion, so that they had climaxed together. He enjoyed her company and particularly her caring for him. He realised that it was now reciprocated and he felt peace within himself.

He knew her ring size from when he purchased the wedding ring in Newport. It was O and he had searched diligently recently for an engagement ring. He had saved money from his temporary work and found a ring that he thought would make Veronica happy. It was from a new antique shop that had been recently opened in Cowes. There had been several from which to choose on just one tray, but he liked the one he felt was right, which was a ruby surrounded by diamonds.

He gave Veronica the box, still on one knee.

She opened it and exclaimed with joy. Stuart put it over her wedding band onto her finger.

"I give you this," he said, "With all the love that I feel for you. I cannot put into words how grateful I am to you. You have made me a whole person at last."

Veronica looked at the ring and smiled. "I will buy you a ring as well," she said. "But we don't really need them to bind us together. We have bonded and will face life together now."

Stuart felt all his prior angers and resentments drift away. "We will," he agreed. "We have each other."

Chapter 30

Epilogue

F rancesca passed her general certificate of Education and obtained a teaching post in a local primary school. Her mother looked after her daughter whilst she was at work. Stuart did keep in touch with them and always sent a card on the child's birthday.

Annabelle stayed single. He did bump into her one day in a shop but she avoided his eyes and stepped back.

Stuart and Veronica were happy together and went on several cruises.

The Future

We cannot predict what the future holds,
We live from day to day,
Events may come and troubles arise,
But we deal with them on the way.

We cannot be happy in every hour,
We may laugh or shed a tear,
But we deal with what arises,
Each day, each month, each year.

We hope to find happiness,
As we tread along life's path,
We hope that we can sing with joy,
And find much about to laugh.

Courage we need, and courage we'll find,
To keep pace of life quite steady,
To know that if hazards arise,
To deal with them we're ready.

We'll remain stalwart, brave and strong,
Living each day with joyous heart,
So that our life is rich with greatest joy,
Memories good before we depart.